Two Weeks in Paradise

A.D. ELLIS

A.D. ELLIS

ONE

Richard Reginald "Reggie" Ward

"I JUST WANT to make sure you're one thousand percent certain this is what you want," the quiet, gruff voice said from behind the partition in whatever airport terminal gate we'd ended up for a hellacious unexpected layover before the second flight of the day.

Oh.

No.

He.

Didn't.

Ben Stephens may have been the perfect mix of gruff lumberjack and sexy dad bod, and I could admit he was a damn fine carpenter, but the man was *not* going to make his daughter question her marriage to my son.

Hell, no.

We were *on the way* to their small, private tropical destination wedding—if the damn weather would ever stop messing with our flights—and there was no way I was going to stand by and let Mr. Dull and Uncultured attempt to talk Megan out of marrying Jason.

"Dad, we've gone over this a million times," Megan answered brightly with patience I definitely wouldn't have had. "Jason is amazing. He's smart, successful, and, most importantly, he treats me well. We've been together three years and never once have I come home heartbroken over something he's said or done—unlike the other trash I dated way back when."

"I just worry he's not enough—" The words a fire poker jabbing at my anger.

"Careful, Dad, your Lariah is showing," Megan warned.

Ben huffed a frustrated laugh. "You're right. I'm sorry. I trust your judgement."

Had I not been snugged into a hidden corner on the other side of the partition trying to rest as we waited for our plane to board—several hours late, let me point out—I knew I would have seen the signature Ben Stephens grumpy face. Worry line between unfairly perfect brown eyebrows, thin lips set firm, the beginning of crow's feet around his hazel eyes. He'd run a hand over his face and his features would soften as they always did when he and Megan were together.

Living in the same town, having children of the same age dating, it wasn't like I didn't see Ben around. I didn't know him well—and had no desire to—beyond knowing he owned a very successful carpentry business in town, his wife had died a while back, and he seemed perpetually grumpy outside of his time with his daughter. He was also the aforementioned dull and uncultured, but that was a judgement coming from my theater bitch side and maybe not completely fair.

However, if he was going to judge my son, my theater bitch could have her way with him.

Jason was an amazing kid. At twenty-four, he had a solid, well-paying job as a yoga instructor. Adopted at age three, Jason had quickly become *Papa's Boy* and joined my late husband, Scott, in our home gym almost daily. Jason and Scott had a connection through their physical fitness while I'd bonded with my son over his love of graphic novels, comedies, and shoes. While theater was in my blood and it stung a bit that Jason never quite glommed onto it the way I'd hoped he would, I cherished the connection we had over his other loves.

I knew Jason still missed Scott—we all did, he was an amazing man and father, and some days the pain of that loss a decade ago was as fresh and raw as the day we said goodbye to him—I also knew my son's determination to make his yoga business a success was a direct homage to his papa.

Megan said something I couldn't quite catch and Ben chuckled. That girl was a ray of sunshine, always bringing up the mood and making people feel like they made her day just by being around. I'd never known her mother, Lariah, but I'd caught on that Megan was her dad through-and-through—and that we should all be grateful she wasn't anything like her mother. That fact, and knowing Ben even the little bit that I did, made me wonder just what Lariah had been like.

And how Ben had ended up with her.

But those were questions I'd likely never ask because Ben and I were not friends and I didn't expect that fact to change in as little as two weeks.

I'd moved to the small town we all now lived in just before Ben's wife got sick. Megan and Jason had known each other from college and loved the fact we all lived near each other. Despite living in a slightly upsized Mayberry, Ben and I didn't run in the same circles, so I'd never really gotten to know him except through what Jason and Megan said.

And really, there was no reason to know the man. I was deeply involved in the theater community in the much larger next-town-over and Ben had a business to run. I was a gay widower and Ben was a married man with a wife the whole town whispered about. Our only real connection was our kids, but even that had never really brought us together.

When Lariah passed away, I wondered at how Megan and Ben handled it, but asking my son's girlfriend about her dead mother didn't seem like appropriate let's-meet-up-for-dinner conversation. Megan didn't talk about her mom and there appeared to have been no love lost between them.

"Why are you hiding in the corner?" Jason asked, his eyes bright and excited despite the fact we were all exhausted and the trip had barely even begun.

Scrambling to my feet, I hoped to avoid Ben and Megan realizing I'd heard their conversation. No such luck. Both of them rounded the partition, honing in on me. Megan's eyes went wide and she tucked her arm into Jason's.

"Dad and I were just talking about how perfect this trip is going to be," she said. "Perfect wedding, perfect vacation, perfect us."

Jason chuckled. "I love your determination to manifest perfection when we're stranded in the middle of an airport waiting for bad weather to clear so we can actually *get* to our wedding and vacation." My son wrapped his arms around his future wife. "But you're right, perfect us." He kissed her on the nose. "And we're so grateful our dads could be here," he said, turning to Ben and me.

Ben.

The man hadn't stopped glaring at me.

As if it was *my* fault he wanted to bad-mouth my son in public and then get mad when I happened to be within earshot?

No, thank you.

I maybe wasn't going to cause a scene in the airport, but I was glad to know he knew I knew what he'd said about Jason. Maybe I'd bring it up once we got to our tropical locale. A little sun and beach, coconut drink in hand, waves lapping at the shore, and then I'd let him know I didn't appreciate the insinuation Jason wasn't good enough for his daughter.

But I could hold my tongue for now.

If the big lunk would stop glaring at me.

"And we're glad to be here for your special day," I said. "You two are the perfect balance, perfect match. I hope you never forget that you're each *always enough* and together you're unstoppable. A lot of people search their whole lives for what you have, don't take it for granted."

Okay, so maybe I wasn't *totally* able to hold my tongue.

Jason gave me a hug. "Thanks, Dad."

Megan pressed her lips together, trying to hide a knowing smile.

Ben's cheeks colored under his scruff.

Good.

My phone dinged. I pulled it from my pocket just as the kids and Ben did the same. Megan squealed. Jason gave a little whoop. Ben huffed what might have been a sigh of relief. I mumbled, "About damn time."

Our plane was finally at the gate. Once it was unloaded and cleaned, we'd be called to board, and our two-week wedding vacation would begin.

Two weeks.

Two weeks away from home. Away from my routine. Away from work and the handful of people I considered friends.

Two weeks in a warm, sunny, tropical location celebrating my baby boy's wedding. Oh, how I wished Scott could be here for this.

Two weeks with Ben Stephens.

That gorgeous body.

The glare.

The grump.

Two weeks.

I could do it. Heck, we likely wouldn't even see each other aside from attending the small, private beach ceremony.

Ben could rest and relax and entertain himself in paradise.

I planned to soak up some sun, read as many gay romance novels as possible, eat a ton of local cuisine, and recharge my batteries while I enjoyed watching my son embark on his happily ever after.

Two weeks.

It was nothing. A blip. Piece of cake.

I hoped my anxiety appreciated the pep talk I was pouring my heart and soul into.

An entire hour later, we finally boarded the plane.

"Excellent," the flight attendant gushed. "We have you both right here." The attendant gestured toward two seats.

"Oh, no, we're not together," I supplied helpfully.

"Lucky, then," the attendant said through a smile that looked as if it hurt. "Your seats are together. If you'll go ahead and store your bags safely in the overhead, we'll be able to get *everyone* loaded and the flight headed toward your happy, sunny destination."

Ben growled. "Just sit down."

"Is my ticket the window seat?"

"I don't care," Ben said through gritted teeth. "Sit. We're holding up the line and we need to take off."

I didn't particularly *want* the window seat. But Ben *was* taller than me and likely could use the aisle for a bit of leg room. And the sooner I sat, the sooner we could take off. So, I hefted my carry-on toward the overhead bin. Ben's grumble filled my ears as he easily lifted the bag the rest of the way for me and shoved it neatly into the compartment.

"Thanks," I mumbled before plopping down in the window seat.

Ben quickly stored his bag and sat next to me.

The line of annoyed travelers filed past us, chatter

and clatter filling the air. When the attendant scurried by, Ben cleared his throat and gestured.

"Yes, how may I help?"

"We're a bit crammed, any chance there's an extra seat so we could both get some leg room?" Ben asked.

"Unfortunately, we're overbooked. We've had to ask some passengers to take different flights. Definitely no extra seats."

Ben tensed, but he said a polite, "Thanks anyway," before dropping his head on the headrest with a grunt as the attendant hurried by.

"You've at least got the aisle, I'm completely squished over here," I muttered. "Ought to check my seat on the ticket."

"I'm like five inches taller than you, least you can do is let me have an extra few inches," Ben grumped.

"The least I can—" I took a deep, cleansing breath. "You know what, never mind. Let's just get to where we're going and enjoy the trip for the kids."

"Yeah, for the kids. They deserve that."

I held my tongue during the captain's welcome and the attendants' safety speeches. I slipped my earbuds in as soon as I no longer needed to listen to the crew in hopes of distracting myself. I even popped a piece of gum into my mouth—being nice and offering some to Ben as well—to ease the pressure change on my ears as we prepared for takeoff.

But by the time we were well off the ground, I couldn't stop myself.

With a huff, I yanked out my earbuds. "Do you *have* to be the poster child for manspreading?" I hissed.

"Huh?" Ben asked, looking up from the magazine he was flipping through.

I gestured toward his tree trunk legs. Okay, they weren't *that* big, but sitting next to him made me feel small. "I get you're all tough, straight guy, hear me roar and all that, but damn, man. You're all spread out. Bad enough I have to be squished in the corner—"

"And nobody puts *Baby* in a corner, right?" Ben growled. "Also, you *get* nothing about me. Nothing."

"I *get* that it's enough I'm squished over here, but now you've gone and spread yourself out like you own the damn place." He was right, I didn't *know* him, but his close proximity and hulking form mixed with his earlier judgmental words were rubbing me the wrong way.

"Sorry, these seats are uncomfortable and my legs were cramped." Ben at least had the decency to shift and give me a tiny bit of room. "Better?"

I grunted, shoved my earbuds back in, and turned toward the window, grateful I'd brought my travel pillow because I planned to sleep until we landed.

Just had to get through the rest of the flight, a boat trip to the island, and then I only had to see him at the wedding ceremony. With any luck, Ben and I wouldn't see each other until our two weeks were up and we crossed paths from time-to-time in town.

I could do this.

For the kids.

TWO

Ben Stephens

THIS TRIP WAS GOING to kill me.

Not only was I *not* really all that thrilled with leaving the shop and traveling to a hot, sunny locale—honestly, I would have much rather taken an Alaskan cruise, I wasn't much of a beach lover—being stuck with fuckin' Reggie Ward for two weeks was going to do me in.

The man was over-the-top, too much, and dramatic all rolled into a firm, slim, cute little package.

Yeah, yeah, I got it, he was in theater. All of that was kinda just the norm. But damn, did he *have* to constantly bitch and squawk and be...I don't know...*sassy* all the fuckin' time?

His son, Jason, was a good kid. I said kid because Megan and Jason were only twenty-four. When I was twenty-four, I was two plus decades into being brainwashed by my parents and their church. I'd already been forced into an arranged marriage and expected to be the money-maker and protector while my new bride called *all* the shots...and I do mean *all*...but I most definitely wasn't *grown*.

Now, at forty-eight, I knew just how young, immature, and ill-prepared I'd been for marriage and real life. I think it was likely why I ended up in such a bad situation with Lariah—buried so deep I didn't know how to get out of it. My therapist was probably the only person in the world—aside from Lariah herself—who was glad my late wife had even existed because the shit she shackled me with before she left this earth was enough to keep my therapist in billing-hours for the next decade at least.

Anyway, Jason was a good kid. Megan was an amazing kid—yeah, I was biased, but the fact she *could* have ended up like her mother and didn't was a huge win. But they were only twenty-four. They were so young. Naïve. Entering marriage with heart-eyes. I just didn't want them hurt—didn't want my little girl hurt.

I'd always been her protector. From her toxic mother. From the dangerous religion I'd been trapped in since birth. From life. I knew kids had to learn the hard way sometimes, but I'd done what I could to let her learn while still keeping her protected and safe. Was Jason up for that job?

Or did he just think he could take her away from me and they'd go flitting off into the sunset fueled only by dreams and love?

Reggie's snoozing form shifted next to me and the next thing I knew, he was using my shoulder as a headrest. What the hell? Part of me wanted to shove him away, but he was sleeping pretty soundly and that meant he wasn't talking and being annoying.

I could just let him sleep.

But I also wasn't sure how I felt about his soft salt-n-pepper hair tucked into my shoulder, those dark, sparkling eyes hidden by his fluttering lids lined with thick fringes of lashes, and gentle whooshes of air escaping from his pretty pink lips as he slept against me.

I'd had feelings for men before. Hell, I'd practically been in love with the star of our basketball team in high school, but there was no way my family would have accepted that. I'd been required to marry Lariah. Period.

However, that didn't mean I hadn't experienced attraction towards men before.

I just wasn't sure what to do with the fact I found Reggie Ward equal parts sexy as fuck and annoying as hell.

Deciding to save myself from any of his drama, I let the man sleep. I just needed us to land, get to the boat, get to the island, and spend the next two weeks as far away from each other as could be expected in a tropical island paradise when your kids are getting married.

Reggie shifted again about twenty minutes before we landed, shoving his pillow against the window and snuggling in for a few more zzzzs. When the aircraft landed, he kept his earbuds in and didn't say anything. I couldn't tell from his face and body language if he was pissed off, just tired, or a combo of both.

The four of us met up once we'd reached the gate. Reggie slipped his earbuds out as the kids spoke about our next stops.

"Tara and Matt are meeting us at baggage claim," Megan explained. "They landed about an hour ago and already have their bags."

Reggie popped his earbuds back in as the four of us trooped toward the baggage claim area. I watched him sling his arm around Jason as they walked a few feet in front of us. Reggie loved his son and I knew Jason thought the world of both of his dads—he talked about Scott, his father who had passed away and Reggie's husband, a lot and it was clear the kid missed him. Megan had shared a bit that Jason's determination to run a yoga studio was in part because his late father had been a fitness guru and they'd spent a lot of their time together in the gym and learning about how to keep the body healthy and strong.

Jason said something to Reggie and Reggie nodded. I felt a pang of regret for saying anything negative about Jason to Megan earlier—partly because it was mainly just my fear and jealousy speaking, and partly because I was pretty sure Reggie had overheard me disparaging his son. I still wasn't one thousand percent sure this young kid could take care of my baby girl as well as I could, but, as Megan would adamantly insist, she was strong and resilient and could take care of herself. I didn't really doubt that, but I sure was having a damn hard time admitting Jason could take my place.

I needed to apologize to Reggie for what I'd said, but I wasn't sure of the time or place. And what if he *hadn't* actually heard what I said? Bringing it up would just open a can of worms.

Lost in my own head, I realized I'd watched my

suitcase go around twice before grabbing it from the baggage claim and joining the crew.

Megan hugged her friend Tara and Jason slapped Matt on the back in a bro hug. They'd invited their two closest friends to the wedding—when they said they wanted a *small* destination wedding, they weren't kidding. For Megan and Jason, they were more interested in their close friends, their dads, and a two-week vacation than in a large gathering and money spent on food and decorations. They'd decided they wanted to have the memories of their honeymoon with friends and family instead of a few pictures of perfect ribbons, tea lights, and place cards.

I glanced around and found Reggie on his knees.

Fuck.

He was messing with his suitcase, but for some reason, the sight of him knelt down went straight to my dick and I couldn't help the dirty thoughts.

Letting myself think about sex of *any* type wasn't something I was used to thanks to my religious upbringing and Lariah. She'd fucked me up big time in the years we'd been together—or fucked me up *more*. I was working on it and my mental health was getting better, but I still had some things to work through.

Didn't seem to change the fact I was turned on by Reggie down on his fuckin' knees and the images playing through my mind of what he'd maybe be willing to do to me while he was down there.

My head immediately went into berating mode.

You're so dirty.

Such a perv.

Sex addict.

No.

Having sexual thoughts wasn't bad.

Sexual thoughts about other consenting adults were normal.

Sex wasn't dirty.

It was okay to not be interested in sex, but it was also okay to want sex.

No one had the right to make you feel bad or dirty for wanting something as natural as sex.

By the time I'd talked myself out of feeling terrible for thinking of Reggie in a sexual way, our group had shared quick handshakes and introductions before heading toward the shuttle service. The plan was to take a shuttle to the boat and the boat would take us to the island.

Jason took charge, dragging Matt to the little kiosk to secure our shuttle to the boat. Five minutes later, a van pulled up. The driver hopped out, helped us load our luggage, and hurried us into the van. "If we hurry, you'll make this boat. If not, you'll have to kill time waiting for the next one."

Shit.

The way our luck had gone with the flight, I immediately worried we'd be stuck waiting hours for a boat to take us to the island. The tension on Reggie's face, the worry-line between his eyes, made me wonder if he was feeling the same way.

Jason climbed into the front seat with the driver.

Megan, Matt, and Tara filled the middle seat.

Which left Reggie and me to stuff ourselves into the very back seat.

Fuck.

Was this what it was going to be like the whole trip? Reggie and me being forced together by default?

No.

We just had to deal with it to and from. Once we were in this little paradise location, we wouldn't even have to see each other outside of the wedding ceremony and maybe a couple meals.

The very back row two-person seat was actually fairly spacious as far as leg room, but my six-four frame took up a lot of space. I wasn't body-builder fit, but I was broad and thick. I knew I could be intimidating to some people. Recalling Reggie's complaint of *manspreading* on the plane, I did my best to keep to my section of the seat and give him room.

He didn't take up much. Reggie was probably about five-nine and that was maybe being generous. I wouldn't have described him as waifish—he had substance, not like a stiff breeze would blow him over—but maybe *delicate*? He had a firm, sinewy build—he probably did yoga or Pilates or similar. He didn't give off the impression of being weak. Whether nerves or anger or something else, he rattled next to me like a pressure cooker about to go off. Reggie Ward was *a lot*—much of it contradiction— rolled into one fuckin' adorable package.

A package I had absolutely no business thinking about in that way.

I was forty-eight, a widower, a business owner, and a man who had a fucked-up past so deep it would take the next forty-eight years to even hope to dig my way out. My parents, their fucked-up religion, and a narcissistic woman I was forced to call my wife nearly destroyed me. I was in no place to even *think* about another relationship.

That wasn't a relationship. That was hell on earth and it's over.

Staring out the window, I wondered if the baggage I carried from the past would *ever* be truly over. Even if I thought it was a good idea, would I ever be able to move on with someone else? Have a *real* relationship? A healthy relationship? And if the answer to those questions ever turned out to be yes, would I actually be able to get involved with a man? Sure, now that I had accurate labels and the freedom to use them, I'd say I was bi-sexual. But knowing I was bi and actually being in a same-sex relationship weren't synonymous.

Didn't matter. I was on this trip to celebrate my little girl's marriage to the man of her dreams. Megan had escaped Lariah's toxicity—mainly because Lariah hadn't wanted to deal with her; having a child was expected, a status symbol, but she hadn't *wanted* a baby. I'd kept Megan by my side from the moment she was born and we basically co-existed in the house with her mother. If Lariah hadn't gotten sick, I likely would have left the moment Megan went off to college. I knew I would have had Megan's support—hell, looking back, I would have had Megan's support long before that.

Which was why I was traveling to paradise to watch my daughter pledge her heart to Jason. A couple people in town had offered advice about how I shouldn't look at the marriage as losing a daughter, but gaining a son. My head understood I wasn't *losing* Megan, I just hadn't gotten my heart on board yet. And it truly wasn't Jason's fault. Or Megan's. It was likely a side-effect of the hellacious marriage I'd spent so many years drowning in.

Did Megan really want to get herself trapped?

Would Jason treat her the way Lariah had treated me?

What kind of weak, pathetic man was I that I'd let my wife reduce me to what I'd become with her? Even with therapy, would I ever escape the mindfuck she'd saddled me with?

A bump in the road knocked me out of the spiral my thoughts had started down. A result of the brainwashing my parents' church put me through and Lariah's continuation of it in the form of her mental and emotional abuse, my head often became my own worst enemy. The physical manifestation of her abusive nature wasn't something to take lightly, and she *had* injured me more than once, but I was a big guy and the physical hurts had been small. The biggest, most painful scars were unseen—constant voices in my head berating me for being weak, for being this big, tough guy who couldn't even stand up to my parents and wife. I hated the level I'd allowed myself to sink to, but it had happened so slowly I'd been trapped and wounded before I'd even realized it.

Could I have taken Megan and run? Sure. But the marriage had been a financial decision made between Lariah's and my parents. If I had left, I would have had nothing—nothing but a child relying on me. And even though Lariah didn't want Megan, she would have taken me to court for custody—either that, or her parents or mine would have. So, I stuck it out. I kept Megan away from Lariah, made sure she was safe and cared for, and I saved up money. I got myself into therapy, paying cash so as not to alert Lariah, and began to work through the nightmare my life had been ever since marrying my wife —and even before.

Pulling myself out of the negative thoughts, I watched the road go by and thought of the dining room table and chairs I'd work on when I returned to the shop —the one place I'd always been able to take comfort and find peace. Taking control of my head and my heart were new skills I was working on—I'd been conditioned to think I was useless, dumb, weak, and not *man enough* to control anything...my confidence had been destroyed from a young age...and my therapist was working with me to build me back up—but I'd always had confidence in my work.

Creating things out of wood was something I'd always been good at.

My family and Lariah's had a lot of money and the marriage had been a business decision to combine the families' power and finances—I'd never been let in on how it all worked, it was done through the church, *for God*, and to this day, I still didn't understand what had taken place beyond me being forced to marry Lariah.

My money—what I'd been saving up since Megan was born—was *mine* and it was my way out when the time was right.

I remembered clearly the day Lariah slapped me and dressed me down in front of Megan. It was the one and only time my daughter had witnessed the abuse—

although, sadly, she'd picked up on it plenty, even without seeing or hearing it—and something had clicked within me.

No more.

Lariah had torn me down forever, but it was over. My daughter deserved better. At the time—and even now—I wasn't as sure that *I* deserved better, but I trusted myself to do right for my little girl.

I'd been lied to and programmed throughout my formative years to believe I was a worthless, no good, dirty sinner who was nothing without God and the church. If I wanted money, happiness, a future, I had to follow what the church taught, what the church told me to do. My parents not only *allowed* me to be brainwashed, they joined right in. In retrospect, while I *did* blame them, they were just as brainwashed as I was— it was a vicious circle.

When I was told I'd marry Lariah and build a family with her, I didn't question it. Well, not much. For one moment, I thought about the fact I didn't love Lariah—we didn't even really like each other—and my mind went to the guy on the basketball team I'd been crushing on for most of high school. Thinking about him brought on a wave of disgust and self-hatred for my sinful thoughts and desires, but I couldn't make it stop. Did I want to marry Lariah? No. Could I have ever just come out and said I wanted to date a boy? Maybe *marry* a boy? Not way back then.

So, I'd gone along with it. With no way to fight it, not even really understanding I *should* have fought it, I went along. At the time, I was under the impression marrying

Lariah was my only hope of opening my own business and building a family for God.

Within days of the wedding, Lariah started in on me.

Over the next two decades, she broke me down. Mentally and emotionally—she used words, fists, sex, money to control me. Had I not already been in a vulnerable state from my religious upbringing, I maybe wouldn't have been so blind to what she was doing, maybe wouldn't have succumbed to the control so easily. But that wasn't the case, wasn't my life's path.

At least not at that point.

Once I'd literally been slapped out of the nightmare I'd been trapped in for so long—and I'd honestly always wonder what it was about *that* particular slap that sparked something in me—I started planning. I obsessively read every single article and book I could get my hands on regarding cults, brainwashing, deprogramming, narcissism, abuse; you name it, I read it. My therapist encouraged my self-education and worked with me on breaking free from the weight of self-hatred Lariah had shoved me into.

And I worked. I worked like a damn maniac. Lariah hated that I was *just a carpenter*, but it was what I loved and was good at. My parents had never loved my trade, but I once overheard them saying if I was working with my hands, at least I wasn't trying to get my dumb head involved in the family finances.

As I worked and built up my name, I saved every cent. Lariah took care of the money, but I'd secretly worked to set up a separate account. I had half of what I was making deposited into our joint account and half into my secret account. The amount she saw coming in was pennies compared to what our families had, and it was one of the one million things she used to drag me down, but my work kept me away from her and gave me a good name in town, so she didn't fight it.

Nearly every penny Lariah handed to me in a form of an *allowance*—yet another way she kept me under her thumb—I stocked away in my secret account over the years. The money she gave me to *keep her out of my hair* —in regards to Megan—was put aside in a secret savings account.

Megan and I lived frugally, but it was worth it to build up enough money so we could eventually walk away. The day Megan went off to college was the day my plans went into motion. *"Daddy, you need to leave. You need to be happy. The god I believe in wouldn't want you living this way."*

I had every intention to leave. Walk away, never look back. At the time, I wasn't sure if I'd move my shop or try to co-exist in town with Megan, but I knew I was leaving her. Both sets of our parents dying had given me more of an opening. I wasn't happy anyone had died, but having fewer people trying to control my life was a huge help.

Therapy had helped tremendously. Knowing Megan was on my side kept me going. Having our parents out of the picture was a definite boost. And knowing Lariah had lost some of her control over me because I had my own money and I'd educated myself was the final bit of encouragement I needed.

And then she'd gotten sick.

Terminally ill.

At first, I thought she was playing me. One more lie, one more manipulation. But I saw the medical reports, saw the prognosis, saw her slowly start to waste away. I opted to stay.

Not to care for her. No, I didn't want anything to do with her—especially when the few times I did venture to her wing of the house she got so viciously hateful. Lariah had hired herself the best home health care money could buy and was well taken care of in her last days.

I continued to just exist. My business flourished. And I waited for my wife to die. I felt nothing but shame and peace once she was gone—shame over feeling no sadness, only relief. With our parents gone and Megan off at school, I allowed the church to do with Lariah whatever she'd left in her will.

Megan was given a sizeable amount of money. She put it away and vowed to only use it for *good* and for things that would make her mother roll over in her grave.

Surprisingly, I was also given a decent chunk—*too live your pathetic life on* was what Lariah had stated in the will.

The rest went to the church.

And Lariah was buried in the big church's cemetery fifty miles up the road.

Megan and I had skipped the service and spent the day at lunch, a movie, and shopping. Folks likely thought it strange, but we had no desire to be at her graveside. No attachment to the woman who had done her best to ruin us.

The van pulled to a stop. "Looks like y'all made it," the driver said.

I blinked away the memories and focused on unloading the van while the kids chattered excitedly about the island, the weather, the wedding, and all the activities they had planned.

"They seem really happy," Reggie mused as we followed Megan, Jason, and their friends toward the boat that would take us to the island.

"Yeah, they do."

"They're good together," Reggie said. "So much more than *enough* for each other." His eyes caught mine, the message clear in his words, before he sped up and boarded the boat before me.

Damn.

Well, I guess I had my answer. Reggie *had* heard me. And he was pissed.

At least I knew my apology was necessary now.

I followed him onto the boat.

The man in charge was telling Megan and Jason they'd lucked out with their timing because the next two weeks were forecasted to be the best weather of the entire year.

The kids, lost in their excitement over getting married, beamed and gushed over how perfect the trip was going to be. I wasn't sure they saw it, but I caught the man's grin and wink. He was good. Reggie's gaze moved from our captain to mine and I didn't miss the knowing smile.

As the four young people settled in to laugh and watch the beautiful waterscape, I moved to stand next to Reggie, far enough away so as not to be overheard.

"We're heading to a tropical island," I said. "Pretty

sure unless they'd picked two weeks smack in the middle of hurricane season, the weather is always the best of the entire year."

Reggie chuckled. "Yeah, they didn't even notice he was giving them a hard time. I guess when you live in paradise, you have to entertain yourself somehow."

We stood quietly, watching the gorgeous blue-green water as we left the mainland and headed toward our tropical destination.

"Hey, listen, I owe you an apology for what you overheard," I started.

Reggie turned toward me and cocked a brow.

"Okay, I owe you an apology for what I said—even though eavesdropping isn't polite," I tried again.

His cocked brow mixed with a frown.

Fuck.

I wasn't doing this well.

"I'm sorry I said Jason wasn't enough. I'm also sorry you heard me say it. That's not the way I wanted to start our kids' wedding trip. And it's also not true." I ran a hand over my scruffy chin. "I've got forty-eight years of baggage I'm toting around—a lot of it having to do with marriage and toxic relationships—my anxiety over Megan getting married has more to do with *me* than with her. I know Jason is a good kid and he treats her well."

Reggie sniffed. "He is and he does."

"I know. So, again, I'm sorry. It's something I'm working on."

"What?"

I shrugged, warm saltwater air washing over me, relaxing the ever-present tension in my neck and shoulders. "Not letting my past fuck up my present and my future."

Reggie studied me and nodded. "Sounds like it's a work in progress."

"Definitely."

He gave a soft grin. "I get it. Scott and I weren't perfect. Even though he's been gone ten years, his death and some of our stupid shit still messes with me."

"Yeah," I muttered. "Mine has more to do with her life messing with me rather than her death, but I get it. We've all got baggage and shit to deal with."

"Yep," Reggie said. "Suitcases, carry-ons, duffles, backpacks, you name it, I've probably got it. Maybe in several color options," he joked.

As the boat ride continued, Reggie and I separated and spent time on our own as well as chatting with the kids, but I found my eyes drawn to him over and over. He was graceful in his movements, but watching him, I noticed something. He moved constantly. Almost like fidgets, but smoother somehow. Was he nervous? Just liked to keep busy? Needed to move to relax? Being in theater, maybe he just appreciated movement.

When we docked at the island, Megan squealed and I couldn't help but smile. This was her trip, her dream come true, her happily ever after. I was damn proud of her and thrilled to be a part of it—all of the *could have beens* came to mind when I thought of how Megan could have turned out. How, even though I was fucked up and wondered if I'd ever get out of my head, I did a good job with her and kept myself sane *for my daughter* when the hell of living with my wife could have pushed me over the edge.

Sure, maybe I would have rather been in a cold, snowy location instead of a hot, sunny, sandy island, but the trip was what my baby girl wanted and I was so grateful to just be part of her life, celebrating with her on her special occasion.

Two weeks in paradise? I could handle it.

Even though Reggie was dramatic and a bit over-the-top in general, he wasn't a *bad* guy. I could put up with anything for two weeks. Plus, it wasn't like I'd have to spend every waking minute with him. I probably wouldn't even see him once we got to the island.

It wasn't going to be that bad.

THREE

Reggie

"Sɪʀ," the man behind the counter at the tiny resort said, "I can't begin to apologize enough. The misunderstanding was quite unfortunate, and if it was within my power to fix the situation, I most definitely would. We are, of course, refunding the reservation money and comping all drinks for your entire stay, but I can't stress enough that there are simply *no more huts available*."

Ben shoved off from the counter and stalked away.

I pinched the bridge of my nose.

Megan went after her dad and Jason winced as he approached me. "Dad, I'm so sorry. When I called to set up the reservations, I must have referred to you and Ben as *our parents* needing a hut."

I shook my head and patted his shoulder. "And they took *our parents* as being a couple who could share a hut. It's unfortunate, but it's not the end of the world. Ben and I will make it work."

"Are you sure? I can ask if there's a roll-out for Tara and Matt to sleep in our hut..." he hedged.

"Don't even think about it," I cut him off. "You're on your honeymoon. You don't want your friends sleeping in your hut. Ben and I are grown-ups and we can deal for two weeks."

Jason frowned. "What if you," he glanced around and lowered his voice, "you know, wanted to bring someone back to your room? Or maybe Ben meets someone?"

I laughed. "Jay, I didn't come down here to find hookups. If Ben did, we'll work it out. Promise." The thought of hooking up with random guys was so far out of my comfort zone, it was laughable. I'd had sex a handful of times since Scott died. All with men I knew and felt comfortable with. My anxiety couldn't even fathom sex with someone I'd never even spoken to. Plus, I was more the type of guy who wanted something to build a relationship on, not a one-night stand.

"I just feel horrible." Jason's face filled with anguish. "I know this trip has your nerves on edge. I know you and Ben don't really know each other and having to share a room is like your worst nightmare."

"Hey, we're all adults here. Ben and I will survive." I hugged my son close. "Your only job is to get yourself married and spend the rest of your life loving your wife."

"You're the best," Jason mumbled. "I wish Papa was here. Thank you for sacrificing for me."

"Your papa would be so very proud of you. He would have adored this trip and watching you marry the love of your life." I patted his back. "Who wouldn't love two weeks in paradise to celebrate love?"

Jason laughed as he pulled away, wiping at the corner of his eye. "Um, *you*." He chuckled as I frowned. "Dad, you despise traveling. You despise having no routine, no schedule, no agenda. Paradise is laid-back, relaxed, lazy, fly-by-the-seat-of-your-pants—all things that you definitely aren't."

"Well, maybe that's just what I need," I said, trying to sound confident. "I'll try my hand at relaxing and having no schedule. I was just thinking that waves lapping at my toes with a fruity drink in hand sounded like a nice way to spend some time." I wasn't lying, those things *sounded* really nice.

Jason gave me a look that told me he and I both knew relaxing sounded great to me in theory, but I had a really hard time actually following through.

I glanced toward the doors leading to the huts as Ben slammed through them, Megan watching him go. Hoisting my bags onto my shoulder, I gave Jason a smile I hoped was convincing and made my way toward the door.

Ben and I weren't going to like it, but we were just going to have to suck it up. For the kids' sakes.

Hustling to catch up with Ben's long strides, I found him at our hut.

Our shared hut.

In paradise.

Sharing a hut with a man you didn't know wasn't exactly my idea of paradise.

Ben used the little palm tree key to open the door and cursed. "Fuckin' hell," he muttered.

Peeking around him, expecting to see a trashed room, flooded floors, or gaudy décor, I moaned.

"Are they shittin' me right now?" Ben roared. "Not only do they put us together in one hut and have nothing else to offer, but it's a single hut? How in the hell do they expect us to not only share a room but also a bed?"

I pushed past him and picked up the phone. "Hi, yes, this is Reggie Ward in hut fourteen. Mr. Stephens and I were hoping there was a roll-away cot or similar we could borrow? You see, it's bad enough you screwed up and put us in a room together, but we'd rather not have to share a bed."

"Mr. Ward, I can't even begin to express just how sorry I am. Unfortunately, we have several cribs available, but the small number of roll-aways we have in stock have all been loaned out."

"Of course, they have," I said through gritted teeth. "Can you please put us on a waiting list and bring one to fourteen if you get one returned?"

"Yes, of course, sir."

I ended the call. "No roll-aways."

Ben growled.

"Look, I know this is less than ideal, but the kids are so worried this is going to ruin the entire trip." I lugged my bags to the small chair by the window and opened the drapes to let in the gorgeous tropical sunshine. Moving toward the bed, I placed the numerous pillows down the middle. "I think we need to grin and bear it. I get it that you're probably not thrilled to share a bed with a gay man, but I can promise—"

"It has nothing to do with you being gay, Reggie. Get

over yourself." Ben tossed his bags to the floor in the corner. "I just wasn't ready to share a room, *really* not ready to share a bed."

"It's a king-size. We'll put up pillows, stay to our own sides, and everything will be fine. I'm not too much of a flopper and I promise not to maul you, how's that?"

Ben ran a hand over his face. "We really don't have a choice, huh? I don't want to mess things up for the kids."

"It really is our only option," I said softly. "Neither of us wants to go back home and miss their wedding just because of a stupid mix-up."

"Going back home doesn't sound too terrible," Ben grumbled.

I cocked a brow.

"But I'm not going to miss their wedding."

"Okay, then," I said, holding out my hand. "We make a pact here and now that we do what we have to do to make sure the kids' wedding and honeymoon is everything they hoped for it to be."

Ben took my hand and gave it a firm shake. "We can't control everything," he started.

"We'll take care of anything within our control then. Come on, you're a big, tough guy, I'm sure you're used to being in control," I teased, a thrill shooting through me at how much I'd like for Ben to boss me around, get me under him, tell me exactly what he wanted me to do.

Ben snorted in disgust and hauled his suitcase to the bed. "I'm going to shower and tour the island. See you at the wedding tomorrow."

Blinking at his abrupt announcement, slightly bereft

at his lack of conversation, I could only nod. "Yeah, sounds good. Have fun."

While Ben showered, I set to work unpacking, tidying up the room, singing along to my favorite Broadway musical soundtracks as I bustled about. Lost in my own head, the music a comforting buffer between me and the chaos of my mind, protecting me against the breakdown bubbling just under the surface over having to share a room with Ben Stephens—just who was he to get so shitty about having to share a room with me? Was I *that* bad?—I didn't realize Ben had emerged from the shower. After going out to inspect the hut's little attached patio area—it was really nice and would make for amazing evenings sipping drinks, taking in the warm breeze, and listening to the gentle sound of waves lapping at the shore—I walked back into the hut and let out a sound of surprise.

Yanking out my earbuds, I held a hand to my heart. "You scared me."

"Yeah, well, I live here," Ben grumped. "Get used to it. Maybe if you weren't blasting your ear drums out with your music, you would have heard me." He watched me as I rearranged a drawer I'd recently filled, his eyes hot and hard on me. "Do you ever sit still? You're like this rotating pressure cooker, always moving, rattling, about to explode."

At first, I started to balk, to shoot back, to defend, but his words struck something. "Dude, you have no idea." Admitting to my anxiety and constant need to be productive, I waved him on. "Have fun on your tour."

Ben headed toward the door. I sensed his hesitation

right as he reached for the doorknob. "Did you, uh...did you want to come with me?"

"Me?" I squeaked. I wasn't one to get invited to many events outside of our theater group. Why in the world would this lumberjack of a man ask me to tour the island with him? "Why?" I narrowed my eyes, studying him suspiciously.

"Man, it's not like I'm going to chop you to pieces and scatter you in the ocean," Ben said with a huff. "Just thought a tour might keep you busy. You seem to like to stay busy." He shrugged. "No big deal if you don't want to."

"No, I do. I just don't get invited many places. Let me clean up real quick, please?"

"Go ahead," Ben said with a gesture toward the bathroom.

I paused. "Are you wearing jeans to walk around a tropical island?" I studied his jeans, boots, and t-shirt.

Ben grumbled. "Megan got me shorts and sandals, but they look ridiculous."

"You'll be miserable in jeans." I gestured toward his suitcase. "Show me what you've got."

He huffed, clearly not happy about it, but proceeded to pull out four pairs of shorts. Two khaki, a navy, and a floral print. "She said since the hut has a washer, there was no reason for more than these."

"Those are great. You'll be much cooler in shorts. Let's see the sandals."

Ben rummaged through his bag and produced a pair of flip flops and a pair of really nice Birkenstocks.

"Ohhhh," I cooed. "These are *nice*. Definitely the

Birks for walking around the island today." Then I winced. "Unless you've never worn them? Mine always rub sore spots the first few times I wear them."

Ben mumbled something I didn't quite catch, his cheeks pinking.

"What?" I asked.

"I *said* I'd been wearing them around the house lately because Megan told me to get my feet used to them."

"And?"

He shrugged. "I guess they're pretty comfortable."

"Perfect. Pick a pair of shorts—any of them will go with that t-shirt. Give me five minutes." I grabbed my bag and rushed to the bathroom. True to my word, I was washed, rinsed, refreshed, and ready in five minutes—what? I was used to quick changes for the stage.

When I exited the bathroom, the sight of Ben Stephens in island-wear stopped me short. He was breathtakingly gorgeous. While his legs definitely hadn't seen as much sun as his face and arms, his skin had a natural golden undertone that kept him from looking pasty. His pretty, intense hazel eyes studied a spray-can of sunscreen, but my eyes caught on his scruffy chin, my mind immediately imagining the sensation of that rough jawline against my skin.

Inwardly chastising myself for ogling the man I'd just promised not to maul, I cleared my throat. "I'll spray you if you'll spray me?" I offered, tossing my bag next to my suitcase.

Ben's eyes left the SPF and looked me up and down. "Good god," he grumbled. "Bad enough we got put together like a couple in the hut, but do we have to dress like twins?"

I chuckled. "It's island-chic, everyone here will likely be dressed the same," I answered in regards to our khaki shorts, pastel t-shirts, and sturdy walking sandals. "The other option is to don a Speedo and walk around in that all day—maybe do the true *old guy* look and put on an open button-up in a floral pattern."

Ben groaned. "Not that I *have* a Speedo, but god, no. I can't even imagine the chaffing that would come from that."

I couldn't help the burst of laughter. "True. Makes me wonder how some of the guys who opt for the look actually walk around all day without their thighs starting forest fires."

A tiny grin played at Ben's lips. "Okay, let's get the sunscreen on. Any ideas about where to go?"

"I was planning to just wander around today. The wedding is tomorrow, but I figured today I'd get my bearings and make some plans for the rest of our time here."

"Making plans on a tropical island seems..."

I cocked a brow. "Controlling? You're not wrong. I just like to know what I'm doing. *Play it by ear* isn't my thing and my anxiety goes sky-high if I don't have at least *some* idea of what's on the agenda. So, I might not plan every second of my stay, but I at least want to know my options for staying busy."

"Workaholic, huh?" Ben asked as he followed me out the door to the patio.

I shook the can of sunscreen. "Yeah, I definitely stay

busy at work. But it's more than that. I grew up with a narcissistic mother who expected me to be perfect, productive, and prompt at all times. If I wasn't, I heard about what a disappointing, unlovable failure I was. So, staying busy, being productive, never knowing how to just relax and *be* is something I deal with now." I gestured for him to turn around so I could spray his neck and ears. "It's not that I don't *want* to relax, I just really don't know *how* to. It's like this spring wound tight inside of me, constantly telling me I have to be in control, be busy, be productive, when all I really want is for someone else to take control and tell me to sit my ass down and relax." As the words poured from my mouth, I couldn't help but question just what the hell I was doing. I didn't know this man. He hadn't asked to hear my pathetic story. Not to mention, I didn't even *like* the guy. I mean, at least not much. "Wow, I'm *really* sorry. Obviously, the jet lag has caught up with me in the form of telling perfect strangers all about my flaws. Just ignore me." I dropped down to spray his legs and the tops of his feet.

Ben chuckled, but kept quiet for a moment.

When he took the can from me, I thought he'd just spray me and move on, but he spoke, his words gruff. "I get that. Kinda. I grew up without a single ounce of control, so it's not something I'm used to doing—taking control of a situation. There's *a lot* more to it, but I'd like for someone to just step back and tell me to take control. Tell me to make the decisions, take the lead, all of that." He paused, spraying my neck. "The thought of it kinda scares the shit out of me, but it's also something I know I

need. Even if it's just a grocery list or what's for dinner."
Ben sprayed the back of my legs and the tops of my feet.

"You don't make those types of decisions at home?
Now that..."

"Now that my nightmare of a wife is gone?" Ben said,
bitterness lacing his words. "I do, but those decisions are
just for me. Megan's on her own and my choices for
groceries, dinner, movies, all that, those only affect me.
Outside of making sure I kept my daughter happy and
healthy, none of my decisions have ever been for anyone
but me. So, the thought of making choices that affect
someone else—of telling someone else what to do—is
overwhelming, but my therapist says it's something I
need to work on." He huffed out a sigh. "And while we're
on the topic of telling complete strangers all about our
fuck-ups, there ya go, just add mine to the list. Pathetic,
huh? What type of guy tells someone he barely knows
that he has a therapist for god's sake?"

I shrugged, rubbing the sunscreen in. "I mean, I saw
one from time-to-time before Scott died. I saw one
weekly for a while after he died—plus family therapy
with Jason. I still talk to my therapist every three months
now. Nothing wrong with having a professional to talk
to." Part of me leaned toward being offended that Ben
referred to men who had therapists as pathetic, but I
realized he was uncomfortable and maybe not used to
talking with others about a shitty past. Maybe Mr. Dull
and Uncultured wasn't as dull as I'd originally thought.

Maybe.

We walked back into the hut. I put the sunscreen on
the dresser and reached for the small tube of SPF I'd

brought for my face. Leaning over the chest of drawers, I smeared the stick under my eyes, on my cheeks, down my nose, and across my forehead. Handing the tube to Ben, I continued. "I don't think there's anything wrong with wanting to take control. We're in different situations and need different things, but we're kinda in the same boat. Shit from our past shaped who we are and now we have a need for something to help us break free from that and become the men we want to be."

Ben studied his face in the mirror as he applied the SPF, but his eyes caught mine and held.

I shrugged at the scrutiny. "I'm just saying, we're kinda peas in a pod."

His brow cocked.

"What? Okay, maybe not peas in a pod in the traditional sense of the phrase, but we both need something to help us escape a shitty past. You need to take control and I need to give up control." I smeared lip balm on and pocketed it for later. Pulling a lanyard over my head, I clipped the hut key to the keychain and checked to see I had my I.D., credit cards, and cash in my card holder. "I find stuff like this fascinating—maybe not so much when it affects me personally, but it's so interesting to think about."

"What is?" Ben asked, his narrowed eyes studying my lanyard as if it had personally offended him.

"Just the way a person's past can mess so much with who they are. Sounds like we've both got some big shit from way back," I paused, thinking about Ben's bitterness over his late wife and added gently, "maybe even some things from not so way back. Different situations, yet somewhat similar led to us having somewhat similar needs even though they're kinda on opposite ends of the spectrum." I shook my head and snorted out a laugh. "If that even makes an ounce of sense."

"No, it does," Ben said. "I get what you're saying." He eyed my lanyard again. "Where'd you get that? Megan told me to think about bringing one—or getting a fanny pack. I said hell no to the fanny pack and figured my wallet would be just fine, but now I wonder if I should have listened to her."

I glanced down at the card holder around my neck. "I like it better than pockets. I use this one at work a lot. I'm sure we could find one in the gift shop or one of the other little boutiques as we walk around. You should put your cards in mine for now and you can hunt for one today."

Ben studied me, a look of indecision clouding his features.

Realizing I'd just taken control of the situation, I thought through ways to make it right and still offer to let him use my holder until he got one of his own. "How about we help each other with what we both need to work on? I'll try to give up some control, you try to take some control?"

He didn't say anything, just stared, but finally broke from his trance with a nod. As if he'd run the situation through his head and decided it was worth a shot, Ben swallowed and took a deep breath. "Since you've got a lanyard and I'm the dumbass who thought carrying a wallet around a tropical island was a good idea, could I put my cards in yours until I find one of my own?"

I couldn't help the grin that filled my face. "Perfect.

See, that wasn't hard, was it?" I took the cards he handed over and tucked them safely in the little pouch hanging from my lanyard. "Now, let's head to—" I cut off and cleared my throat. "Actually, I'm good with whatever and wherever we end up. Lead the way."

Ben chuckled. "Keep telling yourself that."

FOUR

Den

WHAT IN THE actual hell was I doing? Why had I asked Reggie to walk around the island with me? It was bad enough I had to *share a fucking bed* with the guy—even being stuck in the same room was a nightmare—but now I'd gone and invited him to basically hang out all damn day?

I was not cut out for shit like this. If it wasn't for Megan's wedding, I would have taken the boat back to the mainland, found any flight taking me even close to home, and hightailed it out of paradise. Instead, I was stuck there, sweating my ass off, with Reggie Fucking Ward.

Okay, I could admit that he hadn't been *too* over-the-top after his little hissy over the window seat and my comment about Jason—which, to be fair, he had a right to be angry about. Reggie had actually taken my verbal diarrhea in stride and helped me not feel like a complete loser for spilling my guts to a guy I barely knew.

I didn't look down on other people for going to

therapy or having shit in their past, but I held all of that stuff against myself even though I knew it wasn't all my fault. Knowing Reggie had some of the same baggage, even if our situations had been very different, kinda helped ease my self-loathing.

He was still too much, overly dramatic, and over-the-top, but maybe Reggie wasn't *as* annoying as I'd originally thought.

Gee, look at that. See what happens when you take risks and don't close yourself off from people? You meet someone who might become a friend.

I scoffed under my breath as I held the door to a little shop open for Reggie. *Friend* might be pushing it. *Acquaintance I may not completely detest at least for this two-week period* was likely a more accurate description.

Still. Outside of customers you chat with and your kid, you don't really have friends. It's good to have someone to spend time with. The voice of my therapist echoed in my head. Was he going to hang out and spout advice, encouragement, and therapy soundbites the whole damn trip?

Yes. Yes, I am.

I chuckled to myself because I could just picture Bruce tapping his pen on his knee and grinning broadly from his chair.

Yeah, okay, Reggie could *possibly* be a friend.

But nothing more.

Just because he was gay and widowed, and I was bi and widowed, didn't mean we'd hit it off and fall madly in love. I hadn't come to paradise looking for a relationship.

Reggie's slim form breezed past me, his natural scent

mixing with the coconut of the sunscreen we'd applied, and, despite my determination to *not* think of him that way, I couldn't help the sultry direction my brain took. He was an attractive man. Maybe not super model material, but still a cute little package to ogle—plus, he was strangely easy to talk to—which was surprising as hell, but not at all as weird as I would have thought it to be. My thoughts drifted to what these two weeks sharing space with him were going to be like and my dick immediately decided he was on-board and ready to rumble.

Stop, I told myself. *Just because your bi ass is finally free and willing to check out what's out there doesn't mean Reggie finds you attractive or would even be interested.*

"Score," Reggie said, spinning a rack of lanyards with a smile. "See, I knew we'd find some."

I quickly picked a plain black lanyard with a matching black card holder attached.

Reggie sighed.

"What? Black goes with everything. *Yours* is black," I said, poking at his chest.

"Yeah, but there are so many pretty ones. Mine is what the theater provided. But black is boring."

I rolled my eyes. "Excuse me for being boring. If you want something colorful, get one for yourself."

"Doesn't make sense to buy a new one," Reggie said, plucking a purple lanyard with wild orange flowers on it from the rack and holding it up to the mirror. "I'm just saying, when there are all these choices..." His eyes caught mine. "Ah," he said softly.

"When there are all these choices, black is easy. I get it."

I shrugged. "It's easy, but it *does* go with everything. I can use this some other time if I need one."

"Perfect. Do you want to look around more in here or hit some of the other little shops?" Reggie asked.

"As much as I'm loving the air conditioning, this seems more touristy. I'd rather find that furniture store I saw a sign for." While Reggie was reading a t-shirt, I grabbed the purple and orange lanyard and balled it in my fist with my black one. "And there's a tea shop if you're up for that."

Reggie turned back to eye me. "Tea shop?"

I shrugged, fighting off the urge to shrink into myself as I prepared for a verbal onslaught about how pathetic and weak I was for liking tea.

He's not Lariah, a voice said firmly. *You like what you like and you don't have to justify it to anyone.*

"I love tea," Reggie said with a soft smile.

"Perfect," I said, a flutter of something making it hard to catch my breath for a few heartbeats. "Let me get this and we can head out." Sending up a quick *stay over there* vibe, I paid for the two lanyards, hoping my back blocked the view of what I was doing while Reggie browsed not far behind me.

As we headed out into the sunshine, my eyes squinting in the brightness, I pointed toward a bench. "Let's sit. I'll get my cards and key all set up."

Reggie nodded, smirking at me as we headed toward the bench. "Look at you making decisions and taking control. I like it."

The words held just enough teasing and flirtation to have me smiling as we sat down. "By the end of this trip, you'll wish you hadn't turned me so controlling."

"Can't say I'd mind." At least, that's what it *sounded* like Reggie mumbled and I let my mind wander into dirty territory for just a split second. Feeling like a horny virgin, I pushed my thoughts away.

Thinking about sex isn't wrong or dirty or bad.

Yeah, well, I shouldn't have been thinking about sex with my daughter's future father-in-law. Especially when I had to share a bed with him in just a few hours.

"Here, this is for you. I'm sorry for the shitty thing I said at the airport," I blurted, shoving the purple and orange lanyard toward him.

Reggie's eyes widened. "Oh my god, you're the absolute sweetest. You didn't have to do that, but thank you."

Endorphins rushed through me. I hadn't bought a gift for anyone outside of Megan for years and years—Lariah always belittled anything I tried to buy for her and told me to stop wasting her money on stupid stuff, she'd just buy what she really wanted for herself—and it felt good to see Reggie enjoy the simple gesture.

We spent a few minutes arranging our cards and keys. Reggie rolled his theater lanyard and stuck it in a cargo pocket on his shorts. "Thank you, again," he said, leaning close and brushing a light kiss over my cheek.

Time stood still.

Reggie's face blushed a pretty pink.

I fought the urge to pull him close and ask him to kiss me again and again.

"Sorry," he muttered. "Theater habit."

Shaking my head, I said, "No big deal, I'm glad you like it."

"Oh, I like it," Reggie said with a wink after his eyes traveled quickly up and down my body.

We were talking about the lanyard, right?

Reggie chuckled and stood, holding out his hand to pull me up. "Sorry, I'm a flirty, touchy-feely guy. Tell me to knock it off if it makes you uncomfortable." He dropped my hand and I immediately wanted to grab his again. "I promise I won't get my gay all over you." His words were light, but I heard the bitterness in them.

Wrapping my fingers around his elbow, I steered Reggie into a copse of flowering bushes. "Couple things if we're going to be thrown together this whole trip. One, I don't mind the touching. My therapist says I'm touch-starved. Two, stop with the gay comments. I'm not a homophobe. You being gay doesn't bother me in the least. In fact—"

"Dad!" Megan's happy greeting cut off my words and I dropped Reggie's arm.

As the kids approached, Jason glanced between his dad and me just long enough that I wondered if he'd sensed the same...I didn't know what it was...a vibe? A connection? All I knew was something had changed between Reggie and me between leaving our hometown, the unfortunate airport eavesdropping situation, and our short time on the island.

"So, are you guys having fun?" Megan asked, hooking her arm in mine. "Ohhhh, you gave in and got a lanyard. Love it. It will be helpful, promise."

"We've only been to one shop, but we're heading to the furniture place, the tea shop, and maybe lunch," Reggie said, throwing a look my way at the mention of lunch.

I gave a slight nod. We had to eat, might as well do it together.

Look at you doing friend-like things with friend-like people.

I truly couldn't understand the change in my attitude toward the guy. Maybe there was something about the tropical island that had me all jumbled and being weird.

Twenty-four hours ago, I would have balked at the idea of spending the day with Reggie Ward. Eating lunch with him and the prospect of sharing a bed with him would have sent me into grump-mode.

Not that I was *looking forward* to the awkwardness, but the little bit of time we'd spent together hadn't been *that* bad.

"That sounds sooo fun," Megan said, her perpetual sunshine washing over us. "The four of us are doing a moonlight sailboat tour tonight." She frowned. "It's only for four people, or we would have invited you."

"No worries," Reggie said. "I don't know about your dad, but I know jet lag is going to catch up with me. I'll probably crash fairly early. Remind me again what time we need to be on the beach for the ceremony?"

We spent the next few minutes chatting about the wedding plans.

The kids really had done a great job of planning something small and simple with their focus being on the rest of our time in paradise having fun.

Tara and Matt came along the path and the six of us exchanged pleasantries before the young crew took off on whatever adventures they'd signed up for.

"They really are so good together," Reggie mused. "I'm glad they found each other. Scott would have absolutely loved Megan." He paused with a wistful sigh. "Don't mind me talking about my dead husband. He's been gone ten years, but we were together for a long time. He was such a good-hearted guy and would have *loved* being here with the kids. Scott and I had our issues—although, let's be honest, I definitely had more baggage than he did...he was kinda perfect even when he wasn't—but it's easy to remember just the good and think about how much he would have loved this."

"I don't know if you get tired of *I'm sorry for your loss* like I do—for me, it wasn't really a loss, it was the closing of—not even a chapter, it was an entire book I hadn't even wanted to read—but I am sorry you lost the love of your life."

Reggie smiled softly.

"What?"

He shrugged. "Just those words. *Love of your life.* I loved Scott, we were close, best friends, and he was an amazing husband and father. But one of our big...*issues*... was incompatibility. We worked in all of these perfect ways—fit together like the ultimate puzzle."

"But?"

Reggie chuckled. "We spent some time in therapy over the fact that we weren't compatible sexually."

My brows shot up.

"Don't get me wrong, we enjoyed a physical

relationship and neither of us found our situation a *hardship*, but we each wanted things in the bedroom the other just wasn't able or willing to give. So, some of our arguments and rough spots focused a lot on what we couldn't give each other. The majority of the time we were together, everything was great, but there was always this small missing piece that made us both wonder if we truly were meant to be together. Was he really the love of my life? Was I his? In so many ways, the answer was a resounding yes. But that tiny little hole between us always left me wondering. And I'm sure he wondered too." Reggie leaned in to smell a purple flower before continuing. "We had an amazing life together and I wouldn't change it. I miss him every day. We had long talks before he died about what we each wished for the other. His wish for me was to find that piece that was missing between us." He turned wet eyes my way. "And I want to find it, but I don't know that I'll ever find what Scott and I had *plus* that missing piece. And if I do? I don't know if my heart will survive that kind of love and connection." He wiped at his eyes. "Ignore me. I'm a theater bitch to my core, always gotta bring the drama."

I moved close. "No, it's okay. I've spent my life never being *allowed* to express emotions—I'm learning, slowly. At one point in my life, your words would have made me uncomfortable, but I'm okay with them now." Swallowing thickly, I took a risk—inwardly smiling at how proud Bruce would be of me—and said, "I want that."

"That what?"

"Love of my life. I worry I'm too fucked up to find it. I

worry I'll be so focused on fixing me that I'll miss it. Or I'll find it and not know how to keep it." Staring out at the beautiful tropical flowers and trees, I huffed. "Or the things I want—the things I *think* I want, the things I've only allowed myself to wish for—they'll be too much for that other person to handle and I'll lose them."

Reggie studied me for a while. "I need to apologize."

Cocking my head, I waited.

"I thought you were shallow—maybe not snooty shallow, but just surface-level shallow. And you're not. Not at all." He nodded in the direction of the furniture store and we began to walk. "I think the person you find —the one who catches you, sparks that connection, makes you start to wonder *is this it?*—that person will love you for all the things you want, you could never be too much for your soul mate."

As we approached the furniture store, I digested his words. "You believe in soul mates?"

"I do."

"And Scott was yours?"

"He was," Reggie said. "In all the ways he could be. But I don't think we have just one soul mate in our lives. I think we have as many as we need to fill the holes in our heart as we make our journey from beginning to end."

"Now who's not being surface-level shallow?" I joked, not wanting to think about Reggie's words too much.

This guy was nothing like what I'd expected. He made me think. Challenged me.

Reggie had me wondering *is this it* and that question scared the shit out of me. I hadn't come to paradise looking for forever after, but this over-the-top, too much, dramatic man who I'd so recently thought I couldn't stand had somehow gotten under my skin and had me thinking about things I'd never allowed my heart to even hope for.

Had me imagining what it might be like to embrace who I really was and let myself be with a man.

I wasn't the type for hookups—and yes, I knew I was being presumptuous even thinking Reggie would want something like that with me—but we had the whole vacation.

I had a feeling we were going to have an amazing two weeks in paradise whether my sprouting fantasies came true or not.

But damn, I sure hoped they would.

Now, the question was, was I ready to take control and make my dreams come true?

FIVE

Reggie

"GOD, THIS IS GORGEOUS," Ben said for about the millionth time since we'd walked into the furniture shop. The pieces we'd looked at were amazing and I knew the shop easily brought in huge profits from people who were either knowledgeable about furniture and its value *or* people who wanted the bragging rights that came from owning hand-made, original items from Pieces of Paradise.

Ben had already schooled me on types of wood, both hardwood and softwood. "Each type has a different set of characteristics like color, density, grain, and finish. You have to pick the right wood—it's critical when making furniture—because it helps determine the pricing in addition to restoration, resale, or discarding a piece. Not all woods are created equal." He'd gestured around the shop. "This place uses a variety of top-notch selections. Hardwoods are often more expensive, and they're durable, but not all hardwoods are ideal for furniture. Softwood can be somewhat less expensive and easier to work with, but you have to have the right wood for the type of furniture you're making."

"What are some of your favorites to work with?"

Ben's eyes had taken on a dreamy look as he rambled on and on about pine, white oak, maple, walnut, and cherry woods and all of the pros and cons to each. "I've only had the chance to work with teakwood once," he said as he ran his hand over a teak piece that anyone in their right mind would have *loved* to have in their home. "But it remains a top favorite piece I ever turned out. This rosewood," he'd gone on, trailing a finger over a piece, "is a dream wood I'd love to get my hands on some day."

"Do people ever ask for something made from a wood you just don't want to work with?"

"Yeah, sometimes people are trying to get what they want at the cheapest price, but I won't take a job if it's not something I know will be my very best. I'm pretty good at helping a customer bring their idea to life with a wood that fits the piece and their budget, but if they won't bend on the price or the type of wood, I'll turn it down." He shrugged. "It's my business and I won't have it marred by inferior pieces simply because the customer wants to save money. If they want a table and chairs for that cheap, they don't want my artistry, they want a chain furniture store." Ben winced. "Sorry, that sounds stuck up. Lariah hated—"

"Don't ever apologize for believing in your work and expecting to be paid what you deserve for your art and skills."

Ben's mouth snapped shut and his eyes sparkled. "No one's ever said that to me."

"Then you need to hang around better people."

He laughed. "You're the first person aside from Megan I've ever really *hung out* with. She tells me my work is worth a fair price, but she's biased. Lariah always said I was being prideful by charging what I did—said it was a sin to think so highly of myself."

I bit my lip. "I don't like to speak ill of the dead, and I feel a little weird saying this, but your wife was a total bitch."

Ben's eyes went wide for a split second before he threw his head back and laughed until tears streamed from his eyes. "Oh my god, you don't know how badly I needed to hear that. From somewhere other than my own head, I mean. Thank you."

I hooked my arm in his and pulled him toward a chest of drawers I would have loved to have in my bedroom. "I'm a good judge of character," I said. "Lariah was toxic and I'm glad you're free of her. If I have to, I'll take on the job of reminding you how good and talented and deserving you are. Maybe one day, you'll be able to hear the positives over any of the negatives she left you with."

He was quiet for a long moment before he brought his hand up to cover mine on his arm. "I'd like that. My past is really loud sometimes, it would be nice to have a friendly voice talking louder in my head."

As Ben's scent and heat washed over me, his nearness and strength fanning a flame in my belly, I realized that *friendly* was fine, but I wanted something more.

Way to go, Ward. Get a hard-on for your son's straight father-in-law.

I pushed the thought away and moved from Ben's space to check out a treasure box while Ben beelined toward a rocking chair and started going on and on about the artistry of the piece.

When we'd finally wandered the whole store, Ben asked for a business card and we headed out the door.

"I think I'd love to spend a week watching you work," I said as we headed toward the little tea shop.

"What? Why?" Ben's face screwed up in confusion.

"You're obviously very good at what you do, passionate, artistic, and full of knowledge. I love learning about things and watching you would be very educational," I said with a shrug.

Not to mention, hot, I thought as I allowed myself to imagine Ben's big hands creating art from the wood he worked with. I could almost smell the fresh-cut wood, feel the sawdust under my feet, see the sweat on his skin, hear the tools' distinct noises as he worked.

Taste his lips on yours when he pushes you against the workbench and takes control of your mouth, his big body flush against yours as you whimper under his touch.

Fuck.

I took a deep breath of the heavy tropical air.

What the hell was wrong with me? I didn't usually go panting after straight guys. Maybe there was some aphrodisiac property to the flowers on the island that had me going out of my mind over Ben Stephens.

"I'm going to warn you now, I nerd out a bit about tea," Ben said as we crossed to the tea shop. "Lariah hated tea, hated that I knew anything about it, wouldn't even let it be in the house."

"How do you know so much about it? Also, side note, you nerding out about something won't ever be a problem. I love when people are passionate about the things they enjoy."

"My parents didn't allow me to pick my own books or videos. They kept only church-approved non-fiction titles in the house as far as what I was allowed to read and watch. There were only about twenty fiction titles the church approved when it came to chapter books, so I found myself reading a lot of informational shit. I sometimes snuck into the library at school to browse other books, but I was scared shitless someone would either rat me out or casually mention they'd seen me in the stacks. My parents thought libraries were the work of the devil. Anyway, they had this whole set of books that focused on different topics. Bread, gardening, composting, water purification, crochet, paper making, coins, stamps, cars, and tea—each title contained huge amounts of information about the topic. I read each of the books front to back several times—it was better than sitting at the kitchen table memorizing Bible verses with my father breathing down my neck. The tea one was my favorite. My parents kept only the standard black tea bags around and made only sweet tea. The few times I asked to buy a variety pack at least, I was told I was sinful and not being frugal with my money for God.

"Lariah freaked out once shortly after we were married when I put tea on the grocery list. She wanted to know what type of pathetic man was so weak he needed to drink tea when a strong, black coffee was available. She went on a rampage about how good, God-fearing folks had been drinking coffee for centuries." Ben huffed out a frustrated breath. "I wanted to tell her that tea is actually older than coffee, but I kept that tidbit to myself because she was going berserk. She went on for weeks and weeks about what a sinful, shameful, weak man I was for wanting to bring something as frivolous and pathetic as tea into our home." He shook his head and rolled his eyes. "Now, keep in mind, this is the same woman who would sit on the patio with her daily devotionals and sip sweet tea with her mother, but me wanting to grab some herbals or a simple green tea was my one-way ticket to hell."

I screwed up my face. "Who knew tea was so sinful?"

Ben chuckled.

"I mean, I'm kinda joking, but for real, is there something in the Bible about tea being bad?"

"No, she just didn't like when I tried to make any decisions. It could have started with me putting oranges on the grocery list. Tea wasn't the issue, it was me thinking I had any right to decide."

"That's so messed up. *She* was so messed up. I'm sorry you had to go through that. You should have tea or any other damn thing you want in your house. Hell, if she was still alive, I'd have a hard time not telling her exactly what I think of her."

Ben's eyes clouded. "She had a lot of people completely fooled. No one else really saw what she was like. Well, my parents and hers did, but they didn't care. It was only about the church and the money to them." He took a deep breath as if to clear his head. "When I started to wake up and educate myself, started to distance myself from her, I began keeping a variety of tea in my shop. She never came in there. Megan and I would have tea every morning and night. By the time Megan left for college, we were pretty much living in the shop and Lariah couldn't have cared less. She hated us as much as we hated her."

I bumped his shoulder. "Well, since I *love* tea, I'm ready for another schooling."

Ben wasn't lying when he said he knew a lot about tea. The moment we walked in, not only did he look like a kid in a candy store, his eyes sparkled and he started commenting about all the varieties we came across.

When we reached the end of the first tiny aisle—the shop was super cute and cozy—I grabbed one of the adorable little baskets and handed it to him. "You obviously need this," I said with a wink.

"I can't fit much in my luggage," Ben muttered.

Pointing to a sign that said, *Ask Us About Our Shipping Discounts, The More You Buy, The Higher the Discount.* "Pretty sure they're ready for you."

Ben's face broke into a smile. "I hope they have a crate."

Nearly an hour later—although, to be honest, it didn't feel like it because I'd been entranced by Ben's delight and the information pouring out of him—we finished with the checkout and shipping plans before heading to a very late lunch.

When we left the tea shop, Ben seemed to break from his tea-infused bubble. "Fuck, I'm sorry, I didn't mean to take that long or talk so much."

I truly thought Ben had a lifetime of talking and spending time with people who hadn't appreciated him to make up for and I suddenly wanted to be there for each and every word, every single moment of his healing from his past and moving on with his future.

"No worries, I love that you know so much about tea and I can't wait to try some of the things we bought." We'd shared the shipping charges and arranged for our box to be shipped to Ben's place shortly after we got back home.

"You'll have to come over and we'll have a tea party," Ben said. Then he clamped his mouth shut. "Sorry, that was stupid."

"Nothing you say is stupid," I said firmly, gripping his chin and making him look at me. "Do you hear me? I get that this is kinda weird between us since we were pretty much strangers before this trip, but don't ever think anything you say is stupid. Your thoughts and opinions are valid and you can share them with me anytime." Throwing caution to the wind, I leaned in on my tiptoes and pressed a kiss against his cheek. "And a tea party sounds lovely. I'm an over-the-top gay man who's spent my life in theater, a tea party isn't even half as flamboyant as I can get."

"Sounds like a plan then," Ben said, his cheeks blushing a gorgeous shade of pink. "I'll take care of the details, you just make sure you show up."

"Look at you, taking control, I like it."

Ben bit his lip, his eyes landing on my mouth before he cleared his throat. "Yeah, I'm working on it." He smiled. "And I'm starving, let's eat." He led me to a corner table and ordered two waters as we took our seats.

It was just little things Ben was doing, but they seemed big for the two of us. Me letting someone else determine my plans was something I wasn't used to, but I loved how I could just give up the reins for a bit. Ben was simply voicing opinions, sharing his knowledge, deciding on a table, and asking for water, but I had a feeling those were all things he'd never been encouraged to do—all things he'd been ridiculed for, if I had to guess—and I loved that he felt comfortable enough with me to do them.

We were complete opposites in the way we were and what we needed, but we complemented each other very well.

Things between Ben and I relaxed even more over lunch. Maybe it was the traveling catching up with me, or maybe it was the effect of the island, but I couldn't help being honest with him.

"Before this trip, I thought you were dull and uncultured. I was so very, very wrong," I said, sipping my unsweet mango pineapple tea. "I apologize for that. I can't help but be grateful for our kids—first, because they're so very happy together and second, because this trip allowed me to get to know you on a level I likely never would have thought possible back home."

Ben blinked a couple times, took a long sip of his water, and chewed on the corner of his lip. "I'm not used to this whole open, honest, positive communication thing, it's kinda hard," he said. "But if we're admitting things, I used to think you were too out there, too much, too over-the-top." He shook his head. "Now I know you're just passionate. You're just Reggie."

I laughed. "Thanks. That's actually a compliment."

Ben cocked his head. "Is *Reggie* your real name? I'm Benjamin, but only my parents and Lariah called me that. I've always preferred *Ben* and I used it because I knew it pissed them off."

"Reggie is the only name I go by, but it's not my *given* name." I watched him for a moment, stringing out the unknown.

"Can I ask what your given name is? I won't use it if you don't like it."

"Not very many people aside from Scott and Jason know my given name."

He nodded. "That's okay, I get it. I don't need to know."

I reached for his hand and gave it a squeeze. "I'm just giving you a rough time. I don't mind if you know it—I just don't like to tell people I'm not close to."

Ben stared at his hand and then took another sip of water. Was he disgusted that I'd touched him? Embarrassed? Had I gone overboard insinuating we were close when, before our trip to paradise, we barely knew each other?

"My mother named me Richard Reginald Ward after her father and grandfather. My own father wasn't ever part of my life, so she gave me her last name. She called me Richard, which I hated. When I was old enough to pick a name, I realized that I didn't want to be *Dick*—first, because that was just rough period. Second, the gay boy named Dick wasn't going to be a positive experience.

Third, Dick Ward sounded too much like dickwad." I couldn't help but laugh when Ben choked on his water. "I didn't like Reginald, but Reggie was fun. I opted to go by Reggie at school from about fifth grade on. Mom refused to call me Reggie, but everyone else adjusted easily. So, I avoided becoming Dick Ward the dickwad and stuck with Reggie from then on. I'm only Richard Reginald Ward on legal contracts and such." I cocked my head. "What's your middle name?"

"David," Ben said. "My parents went all out with the Biblical names. That's why they hated that I opted for *Ben* and they refused to call me by that name. I got called Benjamin David when I was in trouble—doing something they claimed was sinful and would send me to hell—so I absolutely despise being called that. It brings back too many shitty memories. Lariah used to think she was funny and would call me *Benny* but I learned that she usually used that name right before she went into a rage spiral. So, I stick with Ben because it's the only form of my name that doesn't have some sort of negative memory associated with it."

God, the shit this guy went through. It was a wonder he wasn't curled in a ball, hiding from the world all day every day.

We spent a glorious hour eating our very late lunch or early dinner depending on how you wanted to look at it. It was truly one of the most relaxing, enjoyable times of my life.

"You seem less...on-edge," Ben said warily.

"How can you tell?" I asked, genuinely curious.

"Less tension in your face, fewer twitches, just an

overall softness I guess. Sorry, that probably sounds dumb."

I gave him a look.

"Okay, not dumb." He smiled wryly. "Just an observation."

I smiled. "You're not wrong."

"Just tired? Or truly relaxed?"

I closed my eyes and did a self-scan, processing how I was feeling. "I think I'm truly pretty relaxed. I'm tired, yeah, but it's been so nice to just let go and have nothing to answer for."

"Good," Ben said. "That's good for you to get out of your head and truly let go."

"What's good for the goose is good for the gander," I teased.

"Yeah, I get that. I'm pretty relaxed. Talking to people isn't usually easy for me, but today has been really good. I think Bruce would be proud of me."

"Bruce?"

His face pinked. "My therapist. He's pretty much the only person who knows all of my shit—I don't tell Megan some of it because no kid needs to know how fucked up their parent is. She's well-aware Lariah was a toxic mess, but I don't want to add to it. So, Bruce hears my issues."

"You're not toxic," I said, ready to defend him.

"No, but my daughter doesn't need to know everything I went through, how it still weighs on me, the way it's possibly fucked me up for life."

I nodded. "I get that. Jason knows Scott and I weren't perfect. It was important to both of us that our son not go into his adult life expecting perfection in his relationships. But he definitely doesn't know about the bedroom stuff—no need to scar the kid."

Ben laughed. "Yeah, I hear that." His words made me think he had some bedroom stories or similar in his past as well. Maybe we'd each get a chance to divulge those secrets and get them off our chests at some point, if it felt right.

My brain tried to analyze that thought. Before arriving on the island, all I wanted to do was see Jason get married, get through the two weeks, and get back to work—back to my schedule, my routine, my predictable life.

But now? Now I was wandering a tropical paradise, buying tea out the wazoo, and wondering if the guy I'd always thought I didn't like would maybe want to swap stories about our sex lives?

So. Damn. Weird.

But even weirder was how I wasn't even feeling too freaked out about it. Okay, maybe a bit, but not like majorly. I never in a million years would have expected Ben Stephens to be a calming presence in my life.

Yet, there we were.

I insisted on paying for lunch and Ben agreed only if I let him get drinks and food for the evening meal. As we walked out of the little café, Ben cleared his throat. "You know, it's funny you said you thought I was dull and uncultured."

"No, it's not. I'm so sorry. I maybe shouldn't have even brought it up, but I wanted you to know I was so very wrong because you're one of the most interesting people I've ever met."

He chuckled. "I don't think I've ever been *interesting* to anyone in my life."

"Well, that's probably just because you don't spend a lot of time with others and you don't open up with them."

"Yeah," he said, amazement filling his words, "what's up with that? It's like I walked onto this island and words just started pouring from me."

I sniffed, pretending to be offended. "Well, *I'd* like to think you were just waiting on the right person to spill your guts to."

He laughed. "I'm sure that was it. Totally. But for real, I *am* pretty uncultured."

As I started to ask him what he meant, we reached the hut just as the kids were locking their doors behind them.

"You guys have fun today?" Jason asked, putting an arm around me as Megan gave Ben a hug.

"Yeah, definitely stop by the furniture store if you get a chance. Really gorgeous stuff," I said. "I've got ideas galore on a bunch of pieces I plan on asking my carpenter friend to make for me."

Ben's cheeks pinked and he cleared his throat. "I'm not *that*—"

"You better not say you're not that good," Megan warned. "Your Lariah is showing," she whispered with a kiss to Ben's cheek. "You're the best."

They showed us the brochure for the sailboat tour they were going on and we said goodbye with best wishes and warnings of being careful, staying together, all that parent stuff.

"What does *your Lariah is showing* mean?" I asked as

we watched the kids walk away. "I've heard Megan say it a couple times now."

Ben chuckled and ran a hand through his hair. "It was something we started when Megan was a teen. Any time one of us was being negative or down on ourselves or hateful or anything, we'd tell the other *your Lariah is showing*. Neither of us wanted to be anything like her, so it was always a good little reminder to check ourselves."

"Ah, gotcha. That makes sense."

We walked into our airy, cool, little hut and both groaned.

"I don't think I realized how tired I was until just now. I need a shower and a nap," Ben said with a yawn. "If I don't sleep a little now, I'll be out before sunset."

"Let's shower, rest, and then we can just hang out on the patio with drinks and dinner tonight. The wedding isn't until late morning, so we don't have to get up at the butt-crack of dawn."

"That sounds perfect. You can shower first."

I grabbed my bag. "I won't take long, just want to get the sunscreen and sweat off."

Once I was done, Ben took his place in the bathroom and I walked out to the little hammock on the covered patio. The breeze was warm, but the overhead fan and oscillating fan stirred the air nicely. I plugged in my phone and climbed into the hammock. I knew I'd have to share the bed with Ben later that night, but a nap on the hammock would be comfortable and stave off the awkwardness for a little longer.

Are you really *dreading sharing a bed with that man as much as you originally thought?*

Okay, fine. Maybe being forced to sleep next to Ben wasn't the most terrible situation I'd ever found myself in. As long as we could avoid things getting weird.

And if things get hot?

I scoffed as the hammock swayed. Yeah, sure, my son's straight future father-in-law was going to get handsy with me.

A guy can dream, I thought as I drifted off to sleep.

SIX
Ben

ONCE WE WOKE up from a much-needed nap, I ordered us some pizza and beer.

"This isn't very tropical island-ish," Reggie said around a mouthful of pizza, "but damn, it's good."

"My parents never ordered restaurant pizza, we always had homemade. It was good, but sometimes, especially as a kid, I just wanted some damn pizza from somewhere other than my own kitchen." I took a sip of the beer. "And once Lariah found out I liked pizza, she decided it was of the devil and banned it from the house. So, now, I order pizza any damn time I want it."

"And beer?" Reggie asked, his pretty pink lips curving around the rim of his can as he took a drink.

"I found a book on all the different types of beer— history, how to make it, the differences between each one —and got super interested in it as a teen," I explained. "I knew it wouldn't be something my parents would allow and, later, I never even broached the subject with Lariah, but one of the first things I did when I started staying in my shop full-time was set up a couple different batches of beer. They never turned out as good as I'd hoped—I'd much rather get a good craft beer from a local brewery than drink my own these days." I took another drink. "But every beer I drink is a big fuck you to my parents and Lariah." Chuckling, I drained the can. "It's almost a wonder I'm not an alcoholic."

"Scott and I used to laugh that it was a good thing I used theater to ease my anxiety." Reggie took another bite of pizza. "If I'd used alcohol or pills for that, I would have ended up dead, I'm sure."

"Theater has been really good for you then?" I asked.

"The best. I love it, I'm good at it, and it gives me an outlet for my worries and fears."

"Being on stage doesn't scare the crap out of you?" The thought of being in front of all those people was enough to have me sweating—the sticky breeze wasn't helping.

"No," Reggie said with a smile. "Once I step on stage, everything goes away. I become that character and none of my worries or regrets even dare to get to me. Now, that doesn't mean they aren't *there*, I'm just able to ignore them for a while. The rush I get from a performance allows me to think through things better. And it's not just when I'm performing. I direct as well—pouring myself into all aspects of the theater is the way I relax and when I do my best thinking. And the schedules are helpful in keeping my life predictable."

"What regrets do you have?" I asked.

Reggie swallowed a bite, his head cocked as if playing back his words and realizing he mentioned regrets. "I don't know if they're regrets so much as wondering if things would have been different—better. Should Scott and I have waited to get married? Waited to adopt Jason? Should I have moved out of my mother's house sooner? Should I have opted for a bigger city with bigger theater opportunities? Would Scott have had better options for his fitness coaching if we'd lived somewhere else?" His words were coming quickly by this point and I wondered if the thoughts were starting him down a spiral.

Without thinking, I placed my hand on his. "I think we all have a lot of what ifs in our life. I know it seems I spend way too much time thinking of should haves, could haves, would haves, all that shit. I could have walked out of my parents' house. Should have refused to marry Lariah. Should have known better about so much in my past. But that's where it all is, in the past. Bruce likes to remind me that I can *learn* from my past, but *dwelling* on it isn't productive."

Reggie's eyes studied my hand on his before he took a deep breath and I removed my hand, immediately missing the warmth of his skin under mine. "What have you learned from your past?" he asked.

"You don't know what you don't know," I said simply. "I know *now* how messed up everything was back then. But *back then* all I knew was what my parents and the church taught me, what they allowed me to know—I did have exposure to *worldly* things at school, but I was innocent, naïve, and my parents kept me as sheltered as possible. Plus, they had people watching me and reporting to them—I never understood *why* or what those people were watching for, but I knew I had to toe the line or I'd be in trouble."

I watched as Reggie dipped a piece of pizza in nacho cheese, obviously the very best way to eat pizza, patiently waiting for me to continue.

"When they said I had to marry Lariah, I didn't know to question it, to fight it. They were my parents, they took care of me, they had my eternal soul in mind and they were matching me with a Godly woman for the good of the church—other kids my age in the church were marrying off, it seemed normal to me even if the thought of being with Lariah soured my stomach." I snorted in disgust. "Knowing what I know now, I get how that sounds like the biggest load of shit and has major red flag warnings everywhere. But I knew nothing back then. They told me it was going to be good for our families, good for the church, would provide me with money to support my family, and they'd support my carpentry business. I know now they only encouraged my carpentry skills as a way to keep me out of the financial stuff. Had I had any knowledge of or reason to look into things, I likely would have figured out there was a lot of corrupt shit going on."

Taking a deep breath, not liking to think of Lariah, I went on.

"Sex with Lariah was a nightmare." I shivered and swallowed the sick feeling I got every time I thought of sex with my wife.

"You don't like sex?" Reggie asked, his words gentle.

"It's not that, she just turned it into a mindfuck." I didn't really want to go any deeper into it right then.

Maybe later. "Lariah was heavily involved in the money scheme through our families and the church. By the time the money situation started getting really deep, I'd realized what a fucked up, abusive, no-win situation I was in and I'd made it my goal to get Megan and me out. Then Lariah got sick. Megan was at school. I stayed and kept building my plan, educating and healing myself, and ensuring my future—my daughter's future—was solid. My parents had passed by that point. They died within months of each other—my dad had a major stroke, my mom wasted away to nothing within months because she'd lost her reason for living, lost the man she served in the name of their god. Their deaths stirred a lot of hostility over the money. I'd removed myself from Lariah and anything to do with the church so I had no idea what was going on with the money, but I knew it was big. Lariah's parents passed away while she was sick—I can't prove anything, and if I never have anything to do with the church again for the rest of my life, it will be too soon, but their deaths were suspicious and I wouldn't doubt that Lariah or someone high up in the church had *something* to do with it. Lariah had too much to gain if her parents died. Others in the church stood to profit too much if Lariah's parents died. They both got mysteriously sick, her mom worse than her dad—hell, maybe her dad planned it and wanted her mom dead, but it backfired. Who knows. Either way, they both went into the hospital with these weird symptoms and never came out. Lariah didn't seem the least bit concerned. Maybe because she was so sick, or maybe because she was in deep and wanted them gone."

Reggie's eyes were wide. "Damn, man, every time you talk about your past, it gets deeper and more frightening. It's amazing to me that you made it out."

"I'm fucked up."

"When I say *we all are*, I don't mean to trivialize your trauma. You've got it in spades and your feelings are very valid," Reggie said, placing a hand on my arm. "I just don't want you thinking you're broken or unlovable or a failure because of the shit you went through."

Without warning, my eyes stung and I popped open another can of beer. "Bruce tells me the same thing, are you sure you're not a therapist?" I joked, hoping the swigs of carbonation would drown the lump in my throat.

Reggie smiled. "I'm not a *licensed* therapist, but I *have* played one on the stage."

We both laughed and I was grateful for the levity he'd brought to the deep subject. The conversation moved from our pasts to the kids, the wedding, and what we wanted to do during our two weeks in paradise.

"I'm going to read as many steamy romance books as I can," Reggie said.

Cocking a brow, I asked, "Not the classics? Books turned to stage shows or vice versa?"

He sniggered. "No, I get enough drama in my job—both from the stories we portray and the people I work with—I prefer a good romance story."

"Why romance?" I held up a hand. "No judgement. I've never read one, just curious."

"Well, first, I like romance stories between two guys." His cheeks flushed and he jutted his chin as if to dare me to say something about that.

"There are romance stories between two guys? See? Yet another thing I didn't know. I *definitely* wasn't exposed to romance in the books I was allowed to read." *Fuck.* Romance stories between two men? I immediately wanted to ask Reggie if I could borrow one of his books. Ever since distancing myself from Lariah, my parents, and the church, I'd allowed myself to explore my attraction to men through online resources, newsletters, podcasts, and porn—and I'd learned quickly there was a definite level system to the types of porn out there; I subscribed to a variety in hopes of something hitting at least somewhere close to reality.

In my healing and exploring, I'd realized that, while I was attracted to women, I felt the pull of attraction more strongly toward men. The fact there were romance novels between two men intrigued me because it meant I'd been missing out.

"There *are* and they're really good," Reggie said. "Okay, they're not *all* really good, some of them are just terrible—as with any genre—but I've read some absolutely gorgeous love stories between men. I like romance because, by definition, it has a happily ever after. Or at least a happy for now and I *need* that in my stories. I need to *know*—no matter what the characters and the couple go through—there's going to be a satisfying happy ending."

"Happy for now?"

"When happily ever after seems a little farfetched or reality sets in and we know nothing is guaranteed, you know? Megan and Jason are getting married and we hope it's the beginning of their happily ever after, but we don't *know* what the future holds. Something may happen. Scott and I were living our happily ever after and then he died. We didn't see that part of our story coming. Happy for now just means they're in love and happy in that moment in their journey. They're living their lives as if it's forever, even though we all know forever isn't guaranteed."

I swallowed the lump in my throat. "So, happy for now is like saying *I love you, let's live our forevers together until we no longer can?*"

Reggie's eyes glistened and he nodded. "Yeah, something like that." He swatted my arm. "Damn, Ben, you're some kind of romantic under that lumberjack exterior."

Chuckling, glad he'd broken through the emotion clouding my head—*I* wanted a happy for now. *I* wanted that forever type of love. Even if it wasn't guaranteed to last a whole lifetime, I still wanted it, longed for it. And feared I'd never find it—I cleared my throat and said, "I don't know that I can be a romantic when romance was definitely not part of what I saw between my parents or what I had with Lariah."

Reggie studied me for a moment. "You see Jason and Megan, they're so sweet and in love. Maybe movies and media aren't the best representation of romance—and fictional romance stories aren't always realistic...which is sometimes why I love to lose myself in them so much—but I think a person can be romantic even if they've never seen it or experienced it." He bumped up against me, the move making me realize the three beers I'd downed had me a bit wobbly. "And you, Ben Stephens, carpenter extraordinaire, father of the bride, lover of tea, beer, and pizza, *you* have a romantic streak." He giggled before taking the last drink of his beer. "You must learn to use your powers for good, not evil. Spread your romantic seed across the world."

I cocked a brow and Reggie dissolved into a fit of laughter.

"My *romantic seed*?" I asked, unable to hide my grin.

"Yes, you must give your romantic seed to all of those longing for love." He collapsed into my side, laughing hysterically. "Ignore me, I'm so buzzed. And sleepy."

I couldn't help but laugh as Reggie, plastered to my side, shook with giggles. Along with laughter however was a jumble of thoughts and emotions steam-rolling through my head. *Romance, longing for love, spreading my seed.* The words had me feeling some sort of way, and I wasn't sure how deeply I wanted to examine the emotions.

Romance was something I wanted. During my time with Lariah, I was in survival mode and didn't even consider a romantic relationship. But, thanks to my years of secret therapy and educating myself, and now being truly free, I wanted that now.

Longing for love was something I knew was true about me. I loved my daughter and she loved me, but my heart longed for something more. Something I'd never had with my parents or Lariah.

The spreading my seed part had icy fingers wrapped around my throat.

Sex isn't bad. Sex isn't dirty. Sex isn't a sin. Kinky

fantasies aren't wrong. The idea of sex with Reggie doesn't make you a bad person.

Thoughts of things Lariah wouldn't allow in our sex life—although, it really wasn't much of a *life*—bombarded me. Did Reggie's words hit that much harder simply because of how messed up Lariah had me in regards to sex, intimacy, procreation, and more?

I had definite ideas of things I wanted to do with a man.

With Reggie.

Fuck.

I was drunk.

No way in hell should I have been thinking those thoughts about the father-of-the-groom.

Spread your seed he'd said.

Fuck and damn.

Damn Lariah all to hell for how fucked up she had me.

I grabbed two bottles of water and drained them both.

It was time for bed.

And I needed to crawl under the covers *without* images of a very sexy Reggie spread out under me, open for me, taking me, *all* of me, in ways I'd never been allowed to experience.

Fuck.

Could I do this for two weeks?

"Oh my god," Reggie groaned. "Come on, big boy, let's head to bed." He stood, swayed, and placed his hands on my shoulders when I grabbed his hips to hold him in place. Those gorgeous eyes gazed down at me, fingers gripping my shoulders, sexy smile on his lips. "Thanks for catching me," he whispered. "And thanks for today. I was really kinda dreading this trip—except for the part where it meant something to Jason—but hanging out with you turned out to be surprisingly fun."

I snorted. "Glad I could be of service."

A little moan escaped Reggie's lips. "Damn, I'm too buzzed to say the things *dying* to pour from my mouth, but I do solemnly swear to revisit them in the early morning dawn and reevaluate if they are worthy of being said when sober." He held up a hand as if taking an oath and then dissolved into more giggles.

Reggie pulled me to stand, both of us swaying like palm trees in the tropical ocean breeze, my hands going back to his hips, his hands finding purchase on my torso. His eyes traveled from my chest up to lock with mine and my knees nearly buckled when Reggie licked his lips. Rising up on tiptoes, he pressed a kiss to my cheek. "We can pretend this never happened, but I need you to know, if you wanted to use our two weeks in paradise to take control of a situation and explore, I'm ready, willing, and able. If this is totally out of line—and who am I kidding, of course, it is, coming on to a straight guy isn't usually how I spend my nights—I apologize profusely. If you're on board, the ball is in your court—do with me what you will."

As badly as I wanted to turn my head, capture his lips, and carry him to our bed for a night of exploration, it felt like a situation that we both needed to be sober for. And a conversation probably needed to be had.

Shifting just enough to press a kiss to his temple, I

mumbled, "Good to know. We should probably sleep off the beers so we don't disgrace ourselves at the wedding."

Reggie giggled and nodded, his soft, warm breath tickling my neck. "Yeah. Sleep sounds good."

As much as I'd dreaded sharing a bed with Reggie, it turned out to be a lot less awkward than I'd anticipated. Probably because we were both so buzzed and sleepy from our long day of traveling that we passed out within seconds.

Somewhere in the night, the wall of pillows Reggie had placed between us earlier in the day found their way to the foot of the bed and the floor. Somewhere in the night, likely because I was on the opposite side of where I usually slept, Reggie and I found our way to the middle of the king-sized bed.

And somewhere in the night, my heart rejoiced and sighed peacefully when my arms reached for Reggie and he snuggled into my chest.

What.

The.

Fuck.

SEVEN

Reggie

Oh.

My.

Fucking.

Gawd.

What had I done?

I woke with a furnace pressed to my back, a throbbing in both heads, and a ghastly memory of coming on to Ben the night before.

And now I was cuddled in his arms, hard as a rock, and having a really difficult time convincing myself I shouldn't just go for broke and beg him to fuck me right then and there—put me out of my misery before I had to wake up and face the fact I hit on my son's straight father-in-law.

He's got you wrapped in his arms, how straight can he be?

He was married for god sake, he probably just misses having someone in bed with him.

You're not the only one with a hard *problem this morning.*

Yeah, Ben's morning wood was pressed against my lower back, but that was just a natural part of waking up. It didn't mean anything.

No, I wasn't going to let this get awkward. We'd had an amazing time the day before. Our kids were getting married that morning. Ben and I had to spend two weeks together in paradise. I'd see how Ben wanted to play it once he woke up and we'd go from there. If he brought it up, I'd need to apologize for my behavior. If he ignored it, I'd just let it go.

And secretly enjoy every single second of sleeping next to him for two weeks.

Well, yeah. Duh.

Deciding it would be less awkward—and less enjoyable, but easing the awkwardness was my goal—if we weren't plastered together when he woke up, I gently slipped from his arms and made my way to the bathroom.

By the time I'd relieved myself and brushed my teeth, walking back into the room to grab my bag, Ben had rolled to his back, the sheet down around his hips. We'd slept in shorts and t-shirt—as one does when forced to share a bed with someone you barely know—but his shorts rode low and his shirt was lifted to expose a tantalizing treasure trail, a stomach I wanted to run my tongue over, and a generous sprinkling of hair my fingers itched to comb through. He wasn't body-builder fit, but he was thick and broad, tiny sparkles of silver peppered in the hair, and he had a body that made me feel like I'd be safe and protected. The bulge in his shorts was enticing and had me worried I was drooling, so I rushed to the bathroom and jumped into the shower.

Twenty minutes later, I was washed, refreshed, and hoped the jack-off-to-your-son's-father-in-law session under the steamy water had taken the edge off enough that I wouldn't make a fool of myself that day.

Ben was awake and making tea when I walked out of the bathroom. The moment I took in his broad shoulders and thick legs, I immediately wanted to climb him like a tree and beg him to do dirty, dirty things to me.

Okay, yeah.

Maybe jacking off to the image of his cock in my mouth and coming in my ass wasn't the best idea.

Talk about the very *opposite* of taking the edge off.

The edge was there.

Sharp, hot, and relentless.

Fuck.

"Good morning," Ben said, his words gruff with sleep.

"Morning," I said, hoping my words sounded relatively normal. "It's wedding day!"

"It's wedding day," Ben said, turning to me with a smile. His eyes roamed up and down me and I worried he could tell I'd recently had my cock in hand as I imagined him fucking the daylights out of me. But he just cleared his throat. "Sleep okay?"

"Great. You?"

He nodded. "You need Tylenol or anything?"

"No, the shower helped." I crossed the floor and tossed my bag down. "Listen, I was going to just go with the flow and see how you played it this morning, but I feel really bad. I don't make it a habit to come on to straight guys, especially not a straight guy whose daughter is marrying my son." I swallowed. Hard. "I'm really sorry about last night." I bit my lip, throwing a glance over my shoulder. "And I'll sleep on the floor if you want—I didn't mean to accost you in your sleep."

Ben cocked his head, a cute little frown playing over his features. "What? You didn't accost me."

"I just feel bad because I knew I was a cuddler, but I didn't mean to end up octopused around you. I'd *never* want to put you in an uncomfortable position."

He shook his head, his cheeks slightly pink. "Honestly, I slept better than I ever have. Maybe it was the beer, the bed, the company, I don't know, but it was great." He took a deep breath. "As for what you said, about the ball being in my court—"

I slapped a hand over my face. "Oh my god, I'm soooo sorry. This is humiliating. If we were at my job, I could be written up for harassment. Please, please know that I'm sorry for being an ass and making you uncomfortable." My stomach dropped and I worried I'd be sick. What in the world had I been thinking saying something like that to a straight guy?

Ben moved closer, the scent of sleep and man engulfing me. "I'm not uncomfortable. I just wanted to tell you—"

A knock sounded at the door.

Grateful for the escape from my humiliation, I opened the door for Jason, my heart soaring at my son's excited grin.

But Jason paused, looked at the bed, pursed his lips,

glanced back and forth between Ben and me, and said, "Everything okay? You guys need anything?" An apologetic look crossed his face. "I really am so damn sorry about the hut mix up and having to share a bed."

Ben put up a hand. "It's not a big deal. We're adults, we can handle it. It's not like your dad's a murderer. Hell, I don't even think he's a conservative," he joked and we all laughed.

"Welllll," I said, holding up a finger and drawing out the word. Jason's eyes glittered and he joined me in saying, "I did play one on stage."

Ben laughed and shook his head. "I handed you that one."

Jason held up a bag of something and a tray of coffee. "Thought we'd bring you breakfast. We've got a surf lesson before the ceremony, so we'll see you there." He placed the bag on the counter where Ben was making tea. "You brought tea? Dad will love you forever."

Something punched me in the gut. What was it about Ben that had me feeling some sort of way? I spent my days with tons of people—most theater jobs weren't solitary—and even counting the very small handful of friendly, consensual, casual sex I'd had over the ten years since Scott's death, I'd never experienced the fire in my belly and intense longing I was fighting for Ben.

Yet, Ben Stephens making me tea had me fluttery and jacking off in the shower.

I thought maybe I liked it better when I saw him as a dull, uncultured lug.

Do you really hate the feelings he's flaming inside you?

No. Not even close. The time Ben and I had spent together was the most relaxed, calm, and happy I'd felt in...well, *years* if I was being honest.

But it was a lost cause.

Right?

Ben was a straight widower and the father of my daughter-in-law.

Even if one of those things wasn't true, would a relationship between us be feasible? We lived in a small town where almost everyone knew everyone.

You live in a fairly liberal area and love will always find a way.

I nearly choked on the sip of coffee I took.

Love?

Oh. My. God.

No, no, no.

I was thinking about sex.

That's all.

No one said anything about love.

That would be absolutely ridiculous.

Jason and Ben were both looking at me as I cleared the coffee from my airway and wiped tears from my eyes.

Besides, I'd sworn no more hitting on the straight guy. I pushed the errant thoughts away and smiled. "Sorry, wrong pipe."

You know which pipe *would be the right one?*

Shut.

Up.

I hugged my son and wished him the best, told him we'd see him at the ceremony, and followed him to the door.

"Don't forget, the ceremony is very small and very casual. Don't dress up and don't expect it to take very long," Jason said. "Go ahead and make any plans you want for the day because we won't be taking too much of your time."

"Since khaki shorts and t-shirts are about all Megan let me pack, it's a real good thing it's casual," Ben said, a grin in his voice as he put the final touches on our tea.

Jason smiled. "Yeah, that was our plan. Nothing stuffy or anxiety-inducing or bothersome on our wedding trip. Relaxed, calm, easy, and fun is the theme." He headed out the door and my heart caught in my throat for the billionth time as I fought being sad my baby was no longer a baby and proud of the man Scott and I had raised him to be.

Once Jason left, Ben and I moved to the patio with our food and drinks.

"Damn, this is the life. Maybe I'll find my own island and set up shop," Ben said on a sigh.

"Perfect. Let me know if you'd like to offer stage shows as entertainment for your customers." I didn't really think I could live *forever* in paradise, but I had no qualms thinking about visiting two or three times a year.

We enjoyed our breakfast and drinks as we chatted about things we could do that day. The soft breeze, salty ocean air, and tropical scents of the island lulled my caffeinated and fed body into a gentle slumber. When I heard Ben shift in his seat, I cracked an eye.

"Go ahead and nap for a bit. I'll set an alarm. We're in paradise, there's nothing to stress about," he said with a wink. "I'll shower in a while and wake you when it's time to get ready."

I smiled and drifted back to sleep. Was that what living with Ben would be like? Someone taking care of me, easing the burden of decisions, relieving the worst of my anxiety? Just being there, a presence and a comfort?

I knew it wasn't possible. Wasn't my reality. But paradise was made for dreaming, right?

Thirty minutes before the ceremony was to start, Ben and I found ourselves barefoot in sugary sand that sparkled like diamonds. We walked along the beach as sea birds floated above.

"You okay?" I asked Ben.

He smiled. "Was just getting ready to ask you the same. You seem a little..."

"Edgy? Emotional? Anxious? A hot mess?" I suggested with a wry smile.

"Yes?" He winced. "I think I'm having the same feelings."

"Wanna talk about it?"

He huffed out a laugh. "Talking about things was something we *never* did in my house growing up. And Lariah would have laughed me out of the house—after belittling me and making sure I felt like complete shit—if I ever brought up wanting to talk about a situation— especially how I was feeling." He took a deep breath of the warm sea air and blew it out. "But Bruce encourages it and I've found it helps just to get the words out there sometimes."

I waited, figuring Ben was gathering his thoughts. We were in paradise with no schedule, I could wait for him to get his head together. After all, we were both feeling some kind of way and it would do us both good to at least attempt to put words to our feelings.

How very *real man* of us, huh? Well, fuck toxic masculinity. The only way society would ever break free from the misogyny was to interrupt the cycle. If Ben and I talking about feelings helped to do that, I was all for it.

"My life was shit until Lariah's treatment of me—" He made a strangled noise. "It's hard for me to say *abuse* even though I know that's what it was. Why are men made to feel like they can't be the ones in an abusive relationship?" He swallowed, his eyes on a point ahead of us. "Lariah's abuse—the one slap, for whatever reason, that one out of many, snapped something inside me and set me on the path to escaping—anyway, my life was shit until that point. I didn't *know* it was shit as a kid or a teen. Once we got married and the abuse started..." he paused again and shook his head, "the physical stuff was bad, but the mental and emotional shit was so much worse. I can still hear her in my head some days. But once we got married, everything went from bad to worse. It took me way too long to figure things out. I'm so grateful that I have Megan as the only good to have come from that nightmare, but I regret all the years I lost to my parents, the church, and Lariah." Ben watched a sea bird swoop down and pluck a fish from the water. "I think my feelings are mostly jumbled today because I'm worried Megan will find herself in a bad situation."

He must have felt me tense beside him because he hurried on. "Not that I think Jason is anything like Lariah. He's a great kid; you and Scott did an amazing job with him."

"Megan is honestly a miracle," I interrupted. "Based on how her mother was and how she *could* have grown up...you did such a good job with her. You're both lucky to have each other."

Ben took another deep breath. "She really is. Things could have turned out so differently, but it's almost like something much bigger than me, much bigger than all of this, knew Megan and I needed each other. Or maybe just that I needed her. I don't like to make a parent's well-being the responsibility of a child, but I think just by being in my life, Megan allowed me to see what was happening and make my escape." He scoffed. "Did it help that Lariah got so sick and died? Did it help that our parents died? Yeah, for sure. But I try not to look at that as an easy way out. I couldn't control any of that."

By some unspoken agreement, we reached a tiny grove of trees on the beach and turned around.

"So, I guess my emotions today are a jumble of seeing my baby grow up and move on without me, worry for her that she'll end up in a bad situation like I did, and, selfishly, what life looks like for me now that I'm not just Megan's dad."

We walked in silence for a while.

"That's a lot. Can I comment on some of it? Or would you rather just sit with your feelings?"

"Are you sure you're not a therapist?" Ben joked.

"We do things like this in theater classes sometimes. We might watch a performance or listen to an actor's breakdown of a character and then we offer critiques. But we only ever offer if it's something they want to hear."

"You can comment," Ben said.

"Megan isn't moving on *without you*," I said. "I understand the feeling, but it's not accurate. Megan and Jason aren't starting a life without us, they're just starting their life together. We're still in their circle. They're not kicking us out in order to have their married life, there's still room for us."

Ben nodded. "My head knows that, my heart's just being dramatic I think."

"Your feelings are valid, but the thought you're losing her isn't accurate," I said. "As for her finding herself in a bad situation like you did, I don't see it happening. First, Jason adores her and would die before he ever treated her poorly. Second, Megan is likely hyper-aware of potentially bad situations—how to recognize them, avoid them, deal with them."

"And I hate that," Ben said. "I wish so badly that she'd never experienced anything that made her aware of abusive situations."

"We'd all like to protect our loved ones from bad shit, but it doesn't always work that way. The negativity in her past is something she can use to grow something positive in her future." I checked my phone to make sure we didn't need to increase our speed. "As for what your life looks like now that you're not just Megan's dad," I said. "You've never been *just Megan's dad*. You're Ben. Many faceted; being a father is only one of those sides. I think this is the time you figure out who you are. You didn't get that chance as a teen or young adult. You've taken huge steps by getting yourself out, educating yourself—we don't know what we don't know...you embraced that and made yourself better—and got yourself into therapy." I hesitated.

"What?"

"This may sound terrible, but I'm glad your parents and Lariah and even her parents are dead. Maybe if they were around you could attempt some sort of closure with them, but I'd be worried they'd just try to keep you down, keep you under their thumb. None of them would like it if they knew you'd figured things out and finally stepped out from the heavy shadow of the church's brainwashing —hell, from what you've said, they likely wouldn't have figured it out for themselves, maybe ever." I shrugged. "I just think you've got all this potential and great things on your horizon, and facing them without the people who brought you so much pain is a lot healthier than them still being in your life."

"But what do I *do* with my future?" Ben asked, his words tinged with frustration and fear.

"What do you want to do?"

He was silent for a long time. "I want my business to remain successful and maybe grow. I love what I do and it allows me a nice lifestyle. I want to be a part of Megan's life—not sure I'm ready to be *Grandpa* yet, but someday that sounds like a nice new position. I've got hobbies and I'll likely pick up a few more."

"But?"

"But it kinda feels like just going through the motions and doing things to keep busy and look like I'm living a fulfilling life."

"So, what would make you feel truly fulfilled?" I asked.

"I want what Jason and Megan have. What you and Scott had. But what am I supposed to do, get on Grindr at forty-eight? I wouldn't have the slightest idea how to handle hook-up sex. Hell, for all I know, I'm terrible at sex—Lariah sure told me I was plenty of times." Ben paused and ran a hand through his hair. "And I want something more than just sex. I'm too old for this shit."

"First, I think you mean Tinder," I said, fighting the smile at Ben's mistake. Damn, wouldn't the men of Grindr be drooling all over themselves if he made a profile?

"No, I mean—" Ben cut off when Megan yelled and waved from the ceremony location ahead of us.

Our conversation shelved for a while, we waved at the kids and headed to take our places with Tara and Matt as guests and witnesses at the tiny wedding.

Megan looked gorgeous in a gauzy white sundress. Jason's khaki shorts and palm-tree-printed button-up made me smile to think of some of Scott's old Hawaiian shirts.

A soft, tropical breeze came in from the salty ocean as the officiant, who introduced themselves as Aries, began.

"Welcome to the union of Jason Ward and Megan Stephens. The couple has asked me to keep this short and sweet because they have an island cruise scheduled," Aries said with a smile.

"What? Wouldn't we all rather be exploring a tropical island or relaxing on a hammock than listening to a droning wedding ceremony?" Jason asked, his grin infectious.

"Plus, who wouldn't be excited about cruising an island on scooters?" Megan added.

"Then let's do this," Aries said. "Although, I may need to be offended later when I replay what you said about my ceremony being *droning*." With a wink, they cleared their throat and started. "We're here on this amazing island today to bear witness to, and celebrate, the union of two gorgeous souls. Megan and Jason have found love together and wish to commemorate that love by declaring themselves devoted and legally bound by marriage. As members of their small, sacred circle of family and friends, I'd like to ask the wedding guests to join hands."

Megan and Jason beamed, joining hands as they waited for us to comply. Having not been part of the wedding planning beyond saying I'd help in any way they needed, I'd had no clue what to expect at the kids' ceremony. However, holding hands with Ben Stephens hadn't been something on my list of possibilities.

Damn, man, you've shared a bed, holding hands should be a breeze.

Biting back my snort of laughter—honestly, thinking about how much of a chuckle Scott would get from the whole situation—I turned to face Ben so we could mimic Megan and Jason and Tara and Matt. Holding out my hands, I winked at Ben's frown. "Promise, it won't rub off on you," I whispered.

He frowned deeper, but grabbed my hands like taking a plunge into an icy pool. "Stop saying shit like that," he whispered back. "I'm not a homophobe."

Ben's hands were big and strong, but not as rough as I'd expected them to be for someone who worked with wood and tools. As I wondered what moisturizer he used, a flash of the meme where colleagues had to join hands during an office ice-breaker and one notices the other's right hand is much smoother than the left. She jokes to him that his right hand is so soft, almost like he only uses lotion on that one hand. Then she realizes what she's implied and he realizes she's connecting the dots. I fought back a hysterical giggle and convinced myself it would be wrong to caress Ben's right hand to see if it was softer than his left.

At least during the wedding.

Shit. Maybe my emotions were getting to me more than I'd originally suspected.

Ben gave my hands a squeeze and caught my eyes. Without a word, his serious expression and the pressure of his warm skin against mine brought down the fluttery zing of anxiety and emotions zipping through me.

Calm.

Ben's touch, his presence, his silent look.

He calmed me.

Put me in place. Not in a bad way. But like he grounded me and gave my heart time to decrease its beating, and my brain time to stop short-circuiting.

All with a look and a squeeze.

Gorgeous *and* the yin to my yang.

How completely unfair.

"I welcome you to renew your love to your partner as Megan and Jason speak their vows," Aries said as I came back to myself. "Make a promise, look toward the future, declare your love. Love comes in many shapes and forms. Love is sometimes unexpected. Sharing your life with someone is not something to take lightly, but when you find a person who fits you perfectly, sharing that love is one of the most beautiful things in the world."

With all three pairs of people holding hands and facing each other, Aries addressed their attention to Megan and Jason. My cheeks were hot and not just from the tropical sunshine, but Ben stared intently at me, his hands gripping mine like a lifeline.

The whole situation was...weird, but not off-putting. Weird as in this man I'd barely known until recently was now someone I'd shared a bed with, bonded with like no one else since Scott, and held hands with while wedding vows were spoken.

For a brief second, I tried to imagine doing this with anyone else in my life, but I couldn't do it. Ben Stephens was completely unexpected, but we'd slotted together seamlessly and there was no one I'd rather be witnessing vows and holding hands with as a tropical island breeze fluttered over our sun-warmed skin.

"Love can be difficult—sometimes it hurts and people find themselves fighting it or being brought down by it," Aries said. "But love can be as easy as breathing when it happens between the right souls. Love is so varied—sometimes it's like a switch is flipped. Other times, it's a marathon as two hearts eventually find their way to each other. Neither way is right or wrong, good or bad, just two examples of how love is different for different people. But I asked Megan and Jason to tell me about how they fell in love and they each told me the same story, separately, I might add. A story of how they met and immediately their heart seemed to know it was in the presence of its other half. For Megan and Jason, love sparked quickly between two souls meant to be together. And now, we'll share in the moment as this couple seals their love, now and forever, with their marriage vows."

As Aries flipped a paper on their tiny notebook, I glanced at Ben. His eyes traveled from staring intently at our joined hands to Megan and Jason—who were smiling broadly and nearly floating away in their happiness—to my eyes. What I saw in the hazel depths was a mixture of happiness, uncertainty, and determination.

I wanted to keep his hands in mine. I wanted to keep his eyes on me. I wanted to be in Ben's life as he grew and healed and found himself.

Could you handle just friends?

The thought felt strange. Not because I couldn't be friends with an attractive man, but because *just friends* wasn't the vibe I got around Ben. But what other option was there?

"The couple has chosen to read their vows rather than the whole *repeat after me* thing," Aries said. "Megan, would you like to begin?"

Megan took the small slip of paper Aries handed her and chuckled, a tear slipping down her cheek. My heart caught as Jason reached to brush it away.

"Jason, I take you to be my husband, my forever friend, confidant, and my love. I vow to honor and respect our relationship, you, and myself as we grow and change together. I cherish what we have together and pledge my heart to you and our love for all the days of my life."

The warm squeeze of Ben's hands around mine was enough to send a tear trailing down my cheek as I watched my son fall even more in love with his wife. The soft brush of Ben's knuckle against my cheek shot something hot and gooey straight to my heart.

"Jason," Aries said, handing my son a scrap of paper.

Jason cleared his throat. "Megan, I knew the moment I met you that I'd marry you some day if you'd have me. I take you to be my wife, my closest friend, the person I tell my secrets to, and my forever love. I will work to always hold our relationship and who we are as individuals in the highest regard. I look forward to sharing our life together and watching as we both become the best versions of ourselves. You are my breath, the rhythm of my heart, and the sunshine in my every day. I pledge my heart to you and our love for all the days of my life."

As Megan giggled through a teary hiccup, Ben gave my hands another squeeze. Pulling my eyes from the happy couple, I brought my teary gaze to Ben's. The same tears flooding my eyes stared back at me in the hazel glow of his.

EIGHT

Pen

IF SLEEPING in the same bed as Reggie had thrown me for a loop, holding hands with him as our kids exchanged vows had taken my breath away.

Ever since crushing on a guy in high school, I'd never doubted my attraction to men—even if I'd never dared mention it to Lariah or my parents, never thought it was something my life would allow. But what I'd felt with Reggie since stepping foot onto paradise was more than just an attraction.

Megan and Jason talked about their hearts immediately recognizing their other half and my entire body sparked at how true those words were. I didn't really understand the *how* of such an instant not-just-physical attraction, and I had no clue what to *do* about it, but I knew I wanted to explore it more.

If Reggie was on board.

Was it even possible? We were very different people. We lived in a small town that wasn't super conservative, but also wasn't super liberal. And our kids had just gotten married. That made us family of sorts.

Right?

And maybe Reggie wasn't ready to move on from Scott.

Plus, I had a shit-ton of baggage. No one in their right mind would want to deal with the crap I'd drag into a relationship with me.

Who says it has to be a relationship? You've got almost two weeks in paradise. Burn up the sheets, live out some fantasies, get a little kinky. No one says it has to lead to dearly beloved and happily ever after.

The niggling thought in my emotionally-charged brain wasn't wrong, but those things weren't me. Burning up the sheets, fantasies, and kinks all sounded great—and I definitely had them and wanted to do them—but my heart wanted more than that.

Maybe it made me a sap.

Pathetic.

Weak.

Less of a man.

Maybe I should just want to fuck around and have fun.

But that wasn't where my heart was.

I wanted to fuck around, have fun, get kinky, all of it.

But I wanted to find love, too.

Whatever that said about me, I didn't care.

I'd spent my entire life being lied to, manipulated, abused, and made to feel like less than dirt. I had a lifetime of being told I was a worthless sinner who would burn in hell to overcome, and I wasn't going to add in feeling bad about wanting to find love.

If Reggie wasn't interested, we'd go back home and move on with our lives.

If he *was* interested, we'd still go back home and move on with our lives, but we'd maybe have a lot of fun doing it.

Are you ready to be in a same-sex relationship?

I fought the urge to roll my eyes as I stared at Reggie's hands in mine. I'd been one of only a few *weird church kids* in my school. I'd been married to a woman the whole town simultaneously feared and sucked up to—the whole time either oblivious to the abuse or talking behind my back about how pathetic I was. Being in a same-sex relationship was absolutely nothing.

"With these rings," Aries said, handing small bands to Megan and Jason, "you signify your love and commitment to each other."

Their hands shook as they took time sliding the rings onto each other's fingers. When Reggie's hands trembled in mine, I glanced back at him and caught another tear trickling down his face. I wanted to pull him close, ease whatever feelings were coursing through him, but I knew that would have been a distraction from the kids' wedding. Instead, I reached up again and wiped the tear from his cheek before gripping his hands in mine and squeezing.

The grateful look in his eyes, the way he breathed a sigh of relief, and the small smile on his lips were all exactly what I needed to know I wasn't wrong about what I felt for him.

If he'd have me, I wanted to be the one who wiped his tears, made him laugh, grounded him, and eased his anxiety. In the past, the thought of finding someone I liked enough to share my shit with, someone who would even *want* to put up with what I brought with me, was scary as shit and I seriously didn't think it would ever happen.

But with Reggie, I didn't get that feeling. We'd clicked almost immediately—once we'd gotten over our preconceived notions and the misunderstanding—and I had no fears over opening up to him. No worries about being my true self around him.

Yeah, we had a lot to learn about each other. My past would maybe bring up issues and Reggie had already let on that he and Scott had dealt with some incompatibility—which could have been anything from parenting to finances to sex to chores and anything in between—but there was such an easiness being around Reggie.

"I now pronounce you married. You may share your first kiss as husband and wife," Aries proclaimed.

A rush of pain and sadness washed over me as I recalled my wedding to Lariah and the nightmare that began shortly after. As I watched Jason kiss my daughter, their teeth clicking together through their teary, happy smiles, I wondered just briefly if a happier wedding was in my future.

No. I wasn't sure I could do that again.

But people had long, happy relationships without getting married.

Right?

Good god, man. Slow it down a bit. Thinking about marriage already?

Reggie's sniffley smile pulled me from my thoughts and I had to bite the inside of my lip to avoid pulling him close and either devouring his mouth or holding him tight —or both. It wasn't the right time or place.

Our little party of six stood around offering hugs and well-wishes, chatting with Aries, and discussing plans.

"You two are sure you're good on your own?" Megan asked. "The travel agent who helped us plan this assured us that your names had been given to all of the activities available and they're covered, so feel free to just let them know you're with the Stephens-Ward party and you should have no problem making reservations." She hugged me and then Reggie. "I feel bad leaving you guys to fend for yourselves."

Reggie and I laughed. "We're grown-ass men," I said. "We can handle ourselves."

"Okay, okay," Megan said with a grin. "You're right. We'll have our phones and we'll try to check in throughout the days so you know where we are and what we're doing."

Jason wrapped his wife in his arms. "We'll see them when we see them. Our huts aren't that far apart." He glanced between me and Reggie, a flash of *something* passing over his face. "Call if you need us and have fun." Almost like a parent sending their kid off on their own for the first time.

We watched the four kids walk away as they headed to change clothes and report to their island scooter tour.

"We could do a tour," Reggie suggested.

"They don't want us—"

"Not *with* them," he corrected. "Just a tour by ourselves. Let's let them get started and then we'll check times."

"Wanna change and get lunch? We can look at scooter tours while we eat."

Reggie grinned. "Perfect."

As we made our way to our cabin, Reggie asked, "What else do we want to do?" Then he froze. "Sorry, that was presumptuous. I don't mean you have to include me in your plans. I'm sure you have plenty you want to do."

I bumped against him. "I don't really want to do all the island things on my own," I said. "If you're willing to be my partner in crime, I'm down." Yeah, yeah, the guy who had been *sure* he'd just grin and bear it a couple days ago was actually looking forward to doing some touristy type things.

I didn't miss that Reggie was the catalyst to the change in attitude.

Reggie gave me a sideways glance and said, "Jason suggested he was sorry about the shared room in case either of us wanted to bring someone back while we were here."

I snorted. *No, the only person I want to get in my bed is the guy I'm already sharing with.* "Nah, that's not really my style." Then I snorted again. "Not that I really know what my style is."

"You haven't dated since Lariah died?"

"No," I said. "Busy working on myself for a long time. I feel more ready now, but I don't see me busting onto the dating scene. Figure if something is meant to be, it will just happen naturally. I have such gut fears of repeating what Lariah and I had, I have no doubt I'll know something *good* when it finds me." My heart fluttered happily with how *good* it thought Reggie was. He was *nothing* like Lariah.

Yeah, but most people weren't like Lariah—that didn't mean they were great people and worth devoting my time, energy, and heart to.

Yeah, but...

I sighed. Yeah, but, Reggie was something else. He was the perfect *right* in all of the wrong my life had seen. I wasn't sure how I knew, but my entire being had absolutely no doubt. Even in the short time we'd spent together, I *knew*.

After a quick refresh in the hut, Reggie and I found ourselves at a little ocean-front café. Under a gauzy awning, watching the waves roll in, we sipped lime-mint water and listened to the waitperson describe the amazing island delicacies available on the menu.

When our food arrived—we'd opted to each get a dish to share—we munched on grilled scallops, shrimp, lobster, crab, the best asparagus I'd ever eaten, and a fresh green salad bursting with a citrusy vinaigrette dressing. While eating, we called the scooter tour place and gave our names as part of the Stephens-Ward party. The man on the phone clicked around a few times, made a few approving noises, and declared we'd successfully booked a scooter tour.

When the waitperson came to take our plates, we opted for orange, pineapple, mango smoothies to go—no alcohol since we'd be operating machinery—and paid our bill.

The day was absolutely breathtaking, but, as we strolled toward the scooter rental location, I wondered if any day in paradise *wasn't* perfect.

"Whatcha thinking?" Reggie asked, bumping his hip into me like we were a couple who took walks in paradise every day.

"How amazing this place is. The weather is so nice."

"Would you want to live here full time?"

I thought about that. "No, I don't think so. I think I'd miss the seasons. And if this was my every day, would I get to a point where it wasn't magical?"

"Agreed. I'd miss the weather back home—don't get me wrong, I'll bitch a blue streak when it's too hot or too cold, but if it was perfect every day, I'd have nothing to complain about."

We chuckled as we reached the scooter place.

"I guess we can reevaluate if we're here when it rains. I can't imagine *every* day is perfect."

"Good afternoon, gentlemen," the man behind the counter said. "Welcome to Paradise Scooters. We have your rental ready. You're in luck, your reservation was for the very last vehicle available today."

"Vehicle? We need two," I said.

The man's face fell. "No, no, the reservation said it was for a couple." He ran his finger down a screen. "Right here. Stephens-Ward party, three couples. Two of the couples have already left on their full-day tour and you got the very last scooter." His eyes met mine with apprehension and curiosity, like he was wondering if we'd throw a fit or just take the damn scooter and be happy we got the last one.

Reggie snorted next to me. "Why are we surprised? They put us in a hut together like we're a couple. Might as well make the best of the scooter."

"Can two grown men fit on it?" I asked, the grumble in my voice sneaking back in despite the perfect weather and great company.

"Yes, of course. The scooters are made for two. We suggest the smaller individual sits in front for the best view. It's up to you whether the front or rear person steers the vessel." The man handed us both a sheet of paper. "Now, sirs, if you'd like to sign the liability forms, we'll get your information and send you on your way."

Last week, I would have refused to do the scooter tour. I would have held tight to Reggie being way too dramatic and over-the-top to spend time with. I would have put way too much thought into sharing a scooter with the man.

Now?

Well, now, I was nearly giddy with the situation. But I'd play it cool.

Once we'd signed the papers, I noticed Reggie's patented anxious look etched on his face. "What's wrong?"

"Just nerves, I guess. I'm sorry we got stuck together again. We don't have to..."

"Shut up," I said with a smile. "I'll drive."

Relief washed over Reggie's face and the way he reacted to me taking control of the situation stirred something deep in my belly.

I climbed onto the scooter and gestured for Reggie to join me.

With a pretty pink painting his cheeks, he maneuvered himself between my legs and took his place on the seat. His ass nestled perfectly between my thighs and I knew it was going to be the best scooter ride of my life.

Holding back the ridiculous ripple of laughter threatening to erupt from me, I reached around Reggie and switched on the scooter. Already loving the way his back pressed against me and his warm scent teased my nose, I allowed my arms to touch him slightly more than necessary. "Ready?" I asked, my words gruff at his ear.

"Yeah," Reggie answered.

Was my brain playing tricks or was his voice slightly breathy?

"Use my legs to hold on if you need to," I suggested, my body wanting to demand he grab my knees just so we were touching as much as possible.

Reggie nodded.

"You good? Comfortable?" I asked. "This okay?"

He cleared his throat. "Yeah, all good."

Reggie's voice was definitely breathy.

Was he as turned on by this as I was?

Or was I being ridiculous? The man had a lot more experience than I did. Sure, I'd been married, but Lariah had made sex a nightmare. And the only physical or sexual experience I had with men was through a variety of porn, reading articles, a couple toys, and my right hand.

Just enjoy it. Flirt. See what feels right.

The self-guided tour around the island was absolutely perfect. Whether it was the weather, the view, the activities, or the company—okay, the company...who'd taken hold of my knees and pretty much snuggled into me...was fuckin' great—I wasn't sure I'd ever enjoyed anything more.

We traveled along the shoreline for about a mile, stopping to watch a pod of dolphins playing. At the suggestion of the map on Paradise Scooter's app, we took a right at the far end of the island and made our way through a lush, tropical oasis in the middle of the island. Stopping for pictures with a gorgeous waterfall and colorful flowers, we finally loaded ourselves back onto the scooter and headed toward the little grocery store we'd seen the day before.

"We can fit a couple bags on the platform at our feet and I can probably hold one," Reggie suggested as we browsed snacks and drinks.

"Wanna make cocktails and light a fire on the patio?"

"Are we in paradise?"

"Yes?" I said, narrowing my eyes.

"Then, yes, definitely cocktails and a fire on the patio." Reggie grinned like a fool and my belly fluttered to know he was having as good of a time as me.

By the time we returned the scooter and made our way back to the hut, I was exhausted from all the sunshine and fresh air.

"Oh my god," Reggie groaned. "How old do I sound if I say I need a shower and a nap before we do drinks by the fire?"

"Well, we can be old together because I feel the same way."

"Can I go first?" Reggie asked. "Promise I'll be quick."

"Take your time, I'll get everything ready. We can take about an hour to nap and then spend the whole evening just enjoying paradise on the patio."

"Paradise on the patio sounds like a country song," Reggie teased, but he kicked off his shoes and grabbed his bag before heading to the bathroom.

Twenty minutes later, I emerged from my turn in the steamy bathroom to find Reggie already asleep. In just a pair of basketball shorts, I slipped between the nice, cool sheets and set my phone alarm for sixty minutes. Ignoring the urge to wrap an arm around Reggie—at least for the time being—I rolled to my side and let the exhaustion of the day overtake me.

NINE

Reggie

"I'M OLD," Ben said the next night as we sat on our patio for what was quickly becoming our nightly drinks by the fire. We'd gone for a sunrise beach walk, taken a snorkeling tour of the island's reef, eaten a glorious lunch, and ended the day with a sunset beach walk and a nap before making our way to the patio. Our days together had quickly become an important piece of who I was and I had no idea how I'd go back to being Reggie without Ben in my life. I didn't want to and I wasn't sure I could. But I had no clue how to say that to Ben without freaking him out.

"I don't get how to play this game," Ben continued. His eyes were glassy, but his words were clear and strong, despite being laced with laughter. "I can't remember whether to drink if I *have* done it or *haven't* done it."

We dissolved into snorts of laughter. "We can just play the old person version," I offered. "We just drink when we want to and answer the questions."

From the neighboring party, the speaker crackled with, "Never have I ever been to church."

Ben's eyes locked with mine and he smirked. Raising his hand like a kid in school, he said, "Grew up in a cult called a church. Definitely been to church. Almost daily until I married Lariah. Wasn't until I started taking steps to distance myself and Megan from Lariah, started learning the zillion and one things I didn't know, that I realized not everyone goes to church, not every believes in God."

I shrugged. "I've been to two church services in my life—outside of a couple funeral services held in churches —we didn't attend church growing up." I chuckled without humor. "Pretty sure my mom was too busy being focused on herself to devote any time to church." Watching Ben, I pressed the conversation. "What's it like?"

"Church?" he asked. "Eh, I can't really speak on it. I'm sure there are a lot of different ones. Probably some really good ones. I just have a lot of bad memories of the one I knew." He stared off into the warm night. "Don't get me wrong. I *do* believe in a higher being, probably even *God*." With a deep breath blown out slowly, he continued, "What I don't believe in, now that I've had enough years to reprogram my brain and educate myself, is a bunch of men taking control and wielding power by terrifying people into following them. Telling people they'll burn in the fiery pits of hell if they don't devote their life to *the church* just isn't something I can get behind. It's power-hungry men wanting control and money and prestige. They get off on people looking up to them. They thrive on scaring people, hurting them, breaking them, manipulating them—all in the name of God." Ben shook his head. "Like I said, I'm sure there are some wonderful churches out there, but my parents' church ruined me for any kind of organized religion."

"What was living in the cult like?" I asked.

Ben huffed. "I think I was one of the lucky ones. We didn't have land or a compound or anything like that. I went to public school—I mean, I was pretty much looked at as one of the weird church kids—and, of course, I learned very quickly not to speak about *anything* I learned at school for fear my parents would yank me out and homeschool me. My parents were among the who's who in the area I grew up—they were elite, popular, the in-crowd—or they thought they were...looking back, I'm not so sure. I wasn't mistreated at school, but the kids there definitely knew I was different, I'm not sure if my parents were as *in* as they thought they were. They seemed to toe the line between fitting in with the social scene and following the church. It really wasn't until we moved and they met Lariah's parents that they got deeper and deeper under the church's control and moved further from the social scene." He took a drink. "For the most part, I was a regular kid—as *regular* as a kid can be in a situation like that. I learned later just how much I didn't know. I can't even imagine what I would have been like if I hadn't been exposed to a lot of things at school. When I started breaking away from Lariah, I realized I was ignorant of so many things. There was so much I hadn't done."

"Like what?"

"We don't have the time," Ben answered sardonically staring into his tropical drink.

"Just a few from the top of your head."

"Been to a Broadway show, slept in the same bed as someone else, kissed someone I *wanted* to kiss, danced with someone—hell, *danced*, period—and don't even get me started on how fucked up I am with sex."

I stared at Ben while my brain tried to process. Closing my mouth before I caught island flies, I started to say something. Stopped. Tried again. And stopped.

Ben chuckled. "See? I told you. Don't get me wrong, I was pretty normal compared to others who grew up in worse situations than me, but I figured out quickly there was *a lot* I needed to learn in order to be a good dad to Megan and get myself out from Lariah's and our parents' control."

"Um, are you comfortable talking about any of that list?"

Ben gave a non-committal grunt. "Sure, I guess. I've spilled more shit to you than I've ever told anyone else. Might as well."

"No dancing?"

"Definitely not. Dancing is a sin—of the devil."

"How very *Footloose* of them," I said.

Ben laughed out loud. "I watched that movie—the original and the remake. There were definitely parts to it that accurately portrayed my life back then."

"Have you danced since breaking free of them?"

Ben smiled softly. "Megan and I used to dance around the kitchen. When she was a baby and toddler, I danced with her while I fixed dinner, when she cried, when I felt lost and alone. If the kids had wanted a traditional wedding, I know she would have insisted on dancing. If we hadn't gotten out—well, first, she wouldn't have been marrying Jason. And whoever she did marry— he would have been approved by the church—they definitely wouldn't have had dancing at their wedding."

"Kissed someone you wanted to?" I asked after a few moments of silence.

"I didn't *want* to marry Lariah. Didn't want to kiss her. I was a horny young adult—convinced I was going straight to hell for jacking off multiple times a day—when they made me marry her."

Focus. I had to focus on what Ben was saying, not on the image of him jacking off.

"It wasn't like she wasn't pretty—we just didn't have that spark. Kissing her did nothing for me. The sex—well, that turned out to be another nightmare."

I cocked my head, desperate to keep him talking. "Were you in love with someone else when you married Lariah?"

Ben's eyes bore into mine over his drink, his Adam's apple bobbing as he swallowed. "Yeah, John Telloway, star of the high school basketball team."

My world stopped spinning.

I swallowed.

Play it cool, I thought.

Had Ben just come out to me?

Swallowing again, I ventured, "Did he feel the same?"

Ben laughed bitterly. "Who knows. He likely had no idea who I was or looked at me like the church kid—by high school, my parents were controlling me more heavily and folks around town knew Lariah and I were *promised* to each other." He shook his head, lost in thought. "It wasn't as if I could have told my family I liked a boy. They likely would have sent me off to conversion camp. But all of this—knowing I was bisexual, learning about conversion camps, learning about sex, the list goes on and on—most of this knowledge came later. As a teen, I didn't have words for it, I didn't know what I didn't know, if that makes sense."

Forcing my wildly beating heart to get itself under control, I chose to tuck away the bisexual part for a while and made us each another drink. "What do you mean you've never slept in the same bed as someone else?" I asked, cocking my brow and glancing toward the bed where we'd shared another glorious afternoon nap.

Ben chuckled at where my eyes had gone. "Lariah insisted on separate bedrooms. She was thrilled when I started sleeping in my shop. She didn't want me anywhere near her room or her bed—unless it was for *marriage bed* type stuff and I'd rather jab my eyeballs out than think about how fucked up she was when it came to sex. Don't get me wrong, I'm into sex, but she definitely messed me up for a while. Therapy has been a lifesaver."

"Are you dating anyone?" I thought I knew the answer. Wouldn't I have seen them around town? And Ben wasn't the type to get all flirty and pressed close on a scooter with me if he had someone else back home.

Right?

He scoffed. "No. Like I said, I'm not against a relationship, but at my age, I just don't see the apps as something I want to do." His eyes caught and held mine. "I figure what's meant to be will happen naturally and I'll know it—I'll grab hold and never let go."

Heat flooded my face. How much alcohol had I consumed? Ben couldn't possibly be insinuating *me*, right? Us? Was there an *us*? Did he want there to be?

Oh, god, please let him be hinting that he wanted there to be an us.

Until five minutes ago, I'd spent every moment I'd known Ben Stephens thinking he was straight. Until this trip, I'd also spent years thinking he was dull and uncultured.

Now, both inaccurate views had been blown to smithereens thanks to our time spent together in paradise.

Sweet baby jeezus, it was a lot for a mind to take in.

I cleared my throat. "Um, Broadway," I said, grasping at anything to ground me. "A lot of people haven't been to Broadway."

Ben chuckled ruefully. "I don't mean I've never been to New York's Broadway. I mean, I've never been to a Broadway show—on actual Broadway or anywhere else. Hell, I wasn't allowed to watch stage shows of any kind— except church-sanctioned ones, so Christmas pageants about the birth of Jesus and things like that."

"My theater-loving soul is breaking in two thinking of all the greatness you've missed," I said, meaning every word. But I smiled and winked. "But I'm also thinking about all of the shows I can introduce you to."

Ben grinned. "Lariah went off on me the one time I mentioned us going to watch a theater production—I think it was one you were in if I remember correctly. We hadn't been married long and I thought she'd enjoy a date night. I was very wrong. She spent a week berating me over the sins of the theater."

"Wow," I breathed out. "She was...a lot..."

He laughed. "When I decided to step away and started therapy and all that, I made a list of shows I wanted to see and set up playlists of Broadway songs. I've watched quite a few online if they're available, but I definitely want to see some live."

"Oh, you're going to see some live. Once we're back home, I'm getting you a season pass and you're coming to watch a show at least once a week." I paused and caught his eyes. "If you want, I mean. No pressure. And you don't have to pick shows I'm in, I just want you to see how great theater can be. We do musicals and plays both."

"It sounds amazing. I'd definitely be interested in that." He winked. "But you don't have to give me a season pass, I can buy my own."

"Perfect. We'll make it happen," I said, wondering if Ben felt even a fraction of the excitement churning in my gut at the thought of continuing whatever this was when we got back home. "Do you have any plays or musicals you absolutely want to see?"

"The popular ones, obviously, but I really just want to take it all in. I'll trust you to steer me toward the greats and the less-known titles." His eyes never left mine as he sipped his fruity cocktail. "Maybe it's the drink talking, but I think we should plan a trip."

I cocked a brow and waited.

"We're widowers and empty-nesters now, we have to keep ourselves busy and our minds sharp," Ben said.

I didn't point out that neither Megan nor Jason had been living at home for at least a couple years.

He continued. "I say we plan a trip to New York to watch at least two Broadway shows." His earnest eyes bore into me as if he could will me to agree.

Like he needed to convince me. Ha.

"That sounds fuckin' perfect," I said, my words catching in my throat.

This.

Man.

He'd thrown me for a loop ever since we stepped into paradise, but his admission of being bisexual had sent me over a cliff. Not that I thought he *had* to like me just because he found both men and women attractive, but the flirting, added to that knowledge, had me thinking all sorts of things about possibilities.

And would a guy suggest a trip together if he wasn't interested?

Anxiety started to worm its way into my veins. That old familiar worry and over-thinking. It was too much.

"It's a deal then," Ben said. "We'll get back home and make plans for a New York trip. The kids will be busy with their new married life. The dads can find ways to keep ourselves busy too." He waggled his brows and we both doubled over with laughter.

Was he flirting again? Or just being silly? Or were we drunk?

Either way, laughing and bonding with Ben was definitely the most fun I'd had in...well, maybe in *ever*.

"How will we ever go back?" Ben asked the next night, his words as soft and warm as the tropical breeze they floated on. "I don't know what I'll do without nightly patio drinks once we get back home."

I smiled as the ocean provided a constant soothing background track and sipped my drink. "We could do drinks back home." The two of us had fallen into a habit of adventuring around the island by day and relaxing on the patio by night. And by *adventuring* I meant we took walks, shopped, enjoyed food, and soaked up the sun. We'd done more snorkeling and scooters, and had plans for boating and walking to the tide pools, but we mostly just took each day at a relaxed pace and enjoyed our time.

Ben grunted. "Wouldn't be the same. We'll both get busy with work. Plus, there's the whole lack of the ocean thing."

We both laughed.

"If we stayed here more than a couple weeks, I'd likely end up a drunk. I don't drink this much at home."

"Same," Ben agreed. "Obviously, drinking was a huge *no-no* growing up. Another sin. And Lariah was *not* on-board with alcohol of any type. I'll have a beer a couple nights a week, but you're more likely to find me drinking tea."

"Love that," I answered, my body and brain as relaxed as I'd ever felt them. Paradise had worked wonders on me—the company hadn't hurt either.

"Even if I could have gotten away with it, I don't think I was ever going to be much of a partier," Ben said.

"Then I was forced to get married and everything went downhill from there. Quiet evenings with a beer or tea are my norm. It's nice to relax after working all day." He paused and sipped from a coconut cup we'd purchased from a touristy giftshop earlier in the day. "I often wondered what married life would have been like with someone else. It couldn't have been worse, but would it have been better?" His question hung in the air, but I got a rhetorical vibe from it, so I didn't answer.

After a moment, I asked, "Would you ever want to get married again?"

"I guess I'm kinda a never-say-never type person, but marriage fucked me up and took away half my life. I can't ever see a time when I'd *want* to put myself through that, but I can't say one hundred percent no." He turned a serious expression my way. "What about you?"

I shrugged. "I don't know. Scott and I had something really good. Marriage wasn't a bad experience for me. I wouldn't mind having someone to share my life with again, but thinking about *marrying* someone else almost feels like being unfaithful to Scott."

"Would he think that?"

I laughed. "Not at all. I'm pretty sure Scott only proposed because he knew I wanted to get married. He wasn't a fan of marriage in general—didn't like where it came from and what it stood for, the patriarchy and all that."

"Sharing your life with someone doesn't *have* to mean marriage. A lot of people have good relationships without that piece of paper."

"Yeah, I know. I think it's more the promises made,

for me at least. I get all romantic and gushy over the declarations of love and promises of forever." I sighed, the flowery breeze and alcohol mixing to make me swoony. "Even though we both know forever isn't promised."

Ben was quiet. Thinking about his marriage?

"You know, just like not all relationships have to end in marriage, not all marriages have to be bad," I offered quietly. "What you went through wasn't the norm. You had religion, greed, control, and mental health issues building the foundation of your marriage—even if you and Lariah had loved each other, it would have been damn hard to grow anything *good* out of that base soil. Add in the fact that there had never been love between you, not even a friendship, and it was a recipe for disaster."

"Yeah," Ben mused. "Guess I just wish things had been different. It feels weird to say I don't regret it when almost every second of my day is spent working through some issue that popped up because of that time in my life, but I can't regret it completely because Lariah gave me Megan. So, if I wish my marriage had never happened, wish I'd known how brainwashed and controlled my parents had me, wish I had walked out on Lariah at the very first sign of trouble, then it's like I'm wishing I didn't have my kid. And she's pretty much the only thing that brought me through that time in my life. Living for her, protecting her, getting out for her—she was my focus, what drove me, what still drives me today."

"I get that. There are some pieces of my past I'm not fond of, but I can't completely wish they didn't happen because then my life wouldn't have played out the way it did."

"Like what?" Ben asked.

"Like dating Scott's roommate."

Ben's eyes went wide. "Sounds like a story."

"He was an absolute douche-bag—but totally hot. I met him in a non-theater class and he wooed me by saying he had a thing for theater boys. I didn't know Scott at the time. This guy and I went out a few times over about three weeks before I met Scott at their apartment one night. I'd gone there thinking I was going to let Sam know I wasn't interested in dating anymore, but I got there and Scott answered the door. Come to find out, Sam had gone out with some other guy and asked Scott to cover for him. Scott refused, told me the whole story, told me I better not go out with Sam again—as if I would have —and invited me to go grab coffee with him. The rest is history." I smiled, lost in the fond memory. "If I hadn't dated douche-bag Sam, I wouldn't have met Scott and had so many great years with him.

"I know it's not the exact same because Sam didn't fuck me up the way Lariah fucked you up. She was a narcissistic abuser, plain and simple. I'd never ask you to put a positive spin on anything she did to you. But you're right, Megan came from that period in your life and it's easy to be grateful for that," I said.

As had become our norm, we sat in the quiet dark enjoying our drinks. Our spoken words hanging between us—not awkward, just there—while we savored the sounds and scents surrounding us.

A nearby hut had a party going and the attendees

were well on their way to getting sloshed. A girl shrieked and another person yelled something about, "That's my life motto," before the whole crowd erupted in howls of laughter.

"Life motto," Ben muttered. "You have a life motto?"

I hummed. "Guess I've never thought about. Nothing marketable," I said with a chuckle. "Probably something about living each day to its fullest—we really don't know when we won't have another chance. Taking risks—my anxiety doesn't love that part, but taking risks can lead to big rewards you never expected. Being true to myself, open and honest. What about you?"

"Yeah, same. Definitely not something I could iron on a t-shirt," Ben joked. "Enjoy each day, find the good. Make the most of my healing. Take control of my life—reach out and grab what I want. For so long, there was no good. I didn't even *know* I could grab what I wanted. Healing has allowed me to see the good and recognize what I want." He paused. "I think one of the biggest things for me is living life and being happy—not thinking about every single action and word being a sin that's going to send me to the fiery depths of hell. I lost so much time, I don't want to create more regrets."

The music next door switched to a more mellow beat and the crowd groaned at what I assumed was a song choice they didn't love. "Wanna play a rebel Kevin Bacon and dance?" I asked, the words spilling from my mouth before my brain could think them through.

"Huh?" Ben asked, glassy eyes studying me.

I stood and held out my hand. "Dance with me."

For one terrible moment, I stood awkwardly at an

audition hearing I didn't get the part. Then Ben smirked and took my hand, standing to face me, his larger build crowding into mine. "Thought I was supposed to be working on taking control?"

"Just giving you an opening."

"Where's your anxiety?"

I shrugged. "It seems to take a breather around you." I held my arms out to my sides. "Take control, I'm yours."

Ben's eyes danced in the firelight and I swore something rumbled in his chest. "I might be terrible at this. I've never really danced with anyone other than a toddler many years ago."

"Come on, don't tell me the big ol' sexy lumberjack doesn't dance around the shop while working with wood," I purred, the alcohol had hit hard and I'd reached the point in the evening when it was time to stop.

Ben chuckled and wrapped an arm around my waist, drawing me close. "Sexy, huh?" he asked, his words sandpaper rough.

"Don't act like you don't know you're sexy as sin," I teased, letting him take my hand in his as we swayed to the music.

We kept an inch between our bodies as we moved. Ben's heat caressed my skin, my body begging for him to pull me flush against him. But I had a feeling the slight tension, the barely-there tremor, and the shallow breaths emanating from the big man were a definite sign to let him take the lead—even if that was at a slower pace than what my horny body longed for.

So, we danced.

The alcohol definitely played a part in lowered

inhibitions, but after the time we'd spent together, I could easily say that being around Ben was one of the simplest, most enjoyable things I'd ever experienced.

And I should have just left it at that. Left it as friends who enjoyed each other's company. We could head back home after two weeks in paradise and see where the friendship took us.

But I wanted more.

The itch under my skin.

The heat between us.

The way the tropical air pressed in, heavy with a flowery perfume and promise of something more.

When the song abruptly changed to something loud and thumping, I swallowed thickly and gave Ben my best smile. "Guess we're done," I said, the words tinged with regret hopefully only I could hear. I rose on tip toes and pressed a kiss to Ben's cheek. "You're a good dancer," I whispered.

Turning to head into the hut, convincing myself that I could clean up our mess tomorrow, I decided bed sounded delicious.

Actually, playing out some hot, sweaty, kinky fantasies with Ben sounded more like what I wanted, but I wasn't about to assume the man wanted anything to do with me—

He grabbed my arm, spun me around, and gripped my chin as he walked me into the hut. "I don't wanna be done," he growled.

"Huh?" I squeaked, the drinks and Ben's scent scrambling my brain.

"Kiss me," he demanded. "Be the first and only

person I kiss because I want to," he murmured against my lips.

Alcohol or not, I wasn't going to miss the chance to taste him. Wrapping my arms around his neck, I closed the space between us and pressed my mouth to his. The first contact stole my breath, every sense overloaded as my brain struggled to catch up and my body screamed, begging for more.

Ben grunted and deepened the kiss. When he hauled me tighter against his body, I whimpered, my lips parting, and he took full advantage, his tongue sweeping inside to dance with mine.

He tasted like sin. Fruity coconut and something deeper, darker, and promising. Ben's heat surrounded me, our lips and tongues mating in a hungry kiss. What he may have lacked in experience, he made up for with searing enthusiasm.

When we finally broke apart, both of us breathing heavily, our hips rocking together, Ben pressed his forehead to mine and closed his eyes. "Taking risks, taking control, no regrets," he muttered. "I don't want to look back on this trip and wish I'd done something about this." He paused, his Adam's apple bobbing, and I gritted my teeth to keep from licking his neck. "I know we're drunk, and I know asking for consent before taking that control we talked about may not be sexy—"

"Consent is always sexy," I interrupted, brushing my lips over his.

"I want this," Ben rumbled, grabbing my ass and thrusting our hips together. "Want you under me, in my arms, around my cock." His words poured over me like liquid fire. "You can say no, can always change your mind, but god, I want you so bad."

"I'm right here," I answered, breathless and fearful I'd come in my pants right then and there.

Ben groaned and pulled me back in for a kiss, his tongue stroking mine as he pressed a knee between my legs. "We're drunk," he warned.

"We're sober enough to be having a conversation about consent," I quipped.

His lips devoured mine as he pushed me toward the bed. "Kissing and hands only." Ben gripped the back of my head and held tight as he consumed my mouth. "At least until we're sober tomorrow."

I didn't want to question it, didn't want to wonder if the morning would bring awkward regrets. I wanted to enjoy and savor and explore. God, the things I wanted this man to do to me.

For a brief moment, thoughts of fights with Scott bombarded me. I'd loved him dearly, but our differences in the bedroom had almost ended us more than once. Would Ben be open to what I longed for in bed? Did he have any kinks of his own he'd want to share?

"Hey, where'd you go?" Ben asked, tipping my chin up. "You okay with this?"

Pushing away the worries—no need to borrow trouble...for now, it was just a quick romp—I nodded. "I'm soooo okay with this," I said.

Don't lie to yourself and don't lie to him. You want more than just sex and you want someone to match you in bed.

Later.

We could talk later.

It wasn't as if my bedroom preferences were beyond wild or really far out there. Just because Scott hadn't enjoyed certain aspects of sex didn't mean anything.

Ben gripped the hem of my t-shirt and pulled it over my head before stripping out of his shirt and shorts. Standing there in just a pair of boxer briefs, the man was the epitome of a thick, sexy dad bod—built solid, a perfect mixture of hard and soft, his broad chest rising and falling in anticipation. Eyeing the wet spot on his gray underwear, I shucked my shorts, very aware of the differences in our bodies—but loving every stark contrast.

The way he towered over me.

His thick build engulfing my slimmer frame.

The hint of a former six pack in his abs compared to my thin torso with the beginnings of a belly.

While I had no real qualms about my own body, I found myself drooling over all Ben had for me to savor. He was solid, something to really hold onto.

"You're gorgeous," Ben murmured, stepping close to kiss me, his hands landing on my shoulders and caressing down my arms. "I wanna spend hours looking at you, touching you, kissing all over this pretty skin."

"We have over a week still," I said, my words airy and light.

When I brought my hands to Ben's chest, he tensed.

"This okay?" I asked, kneading his pecs.

With his eyes closed, head tipped back, Ben nodded. "Yeah, fuck, yeah."

Experimentally, I brushed my thumbs over his

nipples. Ben hissed, a strangled noise escaping his throat before he reached for the waistband of my underwear.

In a flurry of motion, we stripped naked, our rock-hard cocks glistening proudly as we took each other in.

Fuck.

Ben's dick was gorgeous and I wanted to drop to my knees and take him deep to the back of my throat. But he'd said kissing and hands only.

So, kiss his cock.

"This feels like a dream," Ben mumbled, his eyes roaming over my chest, my stomach, my cock. "The best dream ever and I don't want to wake up unless I can wake up and find out it's real." His words caught slightly and my eyes held his. "Never thought I'd get the chance to share this with a man. I've wanted this so badly for so long—with a guy and with someone who doesn't hate me." A humorless chuckle escaped him. "Sorry, didn't mean to bring things down."

Gripping my cock and giving a slow tug, I winked. "Definitely nothing going down for me."

Ben swallowed, his dick twitching. "There's so damn much I wanna do—like a lifetime of shit I wanna do—don't know where to start."

"Do what feels right, we've got days and days ahead of us. Take it slow or move fast, your choice. I'm just enjoying the ride."

"Don't want to just use you," Ben said, a pretty frown filling his face.

"Are you kidding? I'm one hundred percent on board and I'll enjoy anything you want to do. Use me, please."

Ben cocked a brow. "Anything?"

Heat filled my cheeks. "I'll say stop if I don't like it."

"Wanna touch you..." Ben wrapped me in his arms. "Taste you..." He buried his face in my neck. "Get off with you..." He pulled me close pressing our cocks together.

We both moaned and rocked, our lips meeting in a fiery kiss as we rutted against each other.

Ben walked me backwards until we reached the bed. We fell together, my body rejoicing in the heavy weight of Ben on top of me.

"Sorry," he started, trying to roll away. "I'm too big—"

"Don't you dare," I warned. "I love it."

Shifting to the middle of the mattress, we kissed and rocked together, our pre-cum smearing between us.

"Pretty much know nothing here," Ben said, his voice edged with contempt.

Taking his face in my hands, I said, "You know what feels good. You know the man you're sharing a bed with loves everything we've done so far." Pulling him in for a kiss, I whispered, "Wanna feel you come all over me. Mess me up."

"Fuck, Reggie," Ben growled. "If we do this again, *sober*, I want to do more. Take more time. Explore."

"Yessss," I hissed, tipping my head so Ben could kiss my neck, my brain having a hard time concentrating on anything but our leaking cocks rubbing together. "But if we don't get off soon, I'm gonna embarrass myself. Touch me."

Ben propped himself on an elbow and reached between our bodies to take both cocks in his big hand. Trembling as he groaned, slowly jacking us, his thumb smearing the pearls of pre-cum over both our cockheads. Ben closed his eyes and moaned.

"Felt the same way first time I touched a dick other than my own," I said, gently rocking into his big hand, his obvious emotions over our connection going straight to my heart.

"I've never—" Ben started, but stopped. "God, so good."

"Just wait until we start exploring," I said. "If you want..."

Ben let go of our dicks and dropped down, bringing our chests together and crashing his mouth against mine. "I want...god, I want." He hoisted my leg up and surged his hips forward, rutting against my cock with his thick length. "Can you come this way?"

I whimpered, already on the brink of exploding.

We thrust and rocked, the hot friction between our bodies spurring us on, our slick pre-cum mixing as we fucked against each other.

Grunts and groans, whimpery cries, and the sound of sweaty bodies rocking together filled the room as the waves crashed in the distance.

"I'm so close," I warned.

"Fuck," Ben growled, "me too."

Losing ourselves to the blissful tangle of limbs, we rutted together for several moments until my balls drew tight. "Gonna come," I gritted out. "Come on me," I begged. "Please."

Ben moved to his knees, jerking his cock as he watched me stroke myself and paint my stomach with long ropes of cum. He groaned and jacked himself harder until his hot release shot all over my chest and chin, the final spurts landing in my belly button.

Just when I thought the big man would collapse onto me, smear our cum-covered bellies together, and kiss me, Ben dropped his cock and sat back on his heels. Covering his face with his hands, he groaned. "Oh my god, Reggie, I'm so sorry. Fuck, I'm sorry. I'll go—"

Quickly enough to make my orgasm-hazed head spin, I moved to my knees in front of him. "Whoa, whoa, nothing to be sorry for. That was amazing. Best sex I've had in a long time, maybe forever." I gripped his hands and pulled them away from his face. "What's up? Talk to me."

"Lariah," he started.

"Time out," I interrupted. "Just need to put it out there. I loved what we just did and I hope we get to do it again. And again." I winked, loving his tiny smile. "And again." I pressed a kiss to the corner of his mouth. "But when we're in the bedroom, especially when cum is still dripping from us and we're both barely outside of the post-nut high, can we please not talk about Lariah?"

He chuckled. "How about I promise I won't use her name? But I kinda have to refer to the past right now." His eyes caught mine. "If you wanna know why I kinda just freaked?"

"I do. No names."

"Can we maybe wipe off first? I'd rather not sleep in a puddle," Ben teased.

Five minutes later, the lights turned off and the room scented by the flowery salt air while the ocean rolled on in the background, Ben climbed back into bed and took my hand.

I wasn't sure why, but it felt like our chat would go best if we were touching, but not face-to-face, so I pushed his legs apart and settled myself in a seated position between his thick thighs. With my back to his front, and Ben's arms wrapped around me, we both sighed as I pulled the light blanket up to our waists.

"So, that was all okay?" Ben asked.

Allowing my head to fall back, I tipped my face up and pressed a kiss to the underside of his jaw. "That was beyond okay. Seriously, I'm not just trying to make you feel good. It. Was. Amazing."

Ben huffed. Relief? Uncertainty? Pride?

"Maybe we get it all out right now? Spill every drop of tea about our pasts? It might help," I suggested.

"Yeah," Ben hedged. "I guess I'm kinda just worried if I tell you everything, you'll realize how fucked up I am—"

"Stop," I said, taking his hand in mine. "We both have pasts. Everyone has a past." It was easier to talk in the dark room with Ben's warm embrace holding me close. "I'm going to be really open and really vulnerable here, I'd like to think what we just shared can continue. And I'm not at all opposed to exploring something more than just sex. Is it kinda crazy that we jumped into this pretty quickly? Yeah, maybe. But we're adults and it's not like we were complete strangers. We had a connection through the kids and, maybe it's just me, but I don't think so, the spark between us has been there from the beginning. It just took an island paradise forcing us together to see it."

Ben nodded, his lips feathering over my cheek. "You're right." He nuzzled into me, his warm strength soothing every part of me. "First, I'm sorry I didn't just straight up tell you I'm bisexual from the beginning. The few times I tried to, we got interrupted. But I don't want it to seem like I was hiding it from you. I've known I found men attractive since my teen years, but didn't really have a word for it until I took purposeful steps away from...*her*. Bi is what I'm using for now, but there may be a better label. I just know I've always thought you were gorgeous—even when I thought you were too much and over-the-top dramatic," he teased. "And getting to know you better just cemented it."

I squeezed his hand. "It's okay. You don't owe anyone an explanation. You like who you like and I'm sorry I assumed anything about your sexuality."

Ben was quiet for several moments and my anxiety nearly drove me to prattle on instead of allowing him to gather his thoughts. When he finally spoke, his words were tinged with a mixture of shame, regret, and anger.

"She was terrible. In so many ways, but the bedroom was maybe the most fucked up." Ben took a deep breath, his chest rising and falling. "As I've worked through things in therapy, I've had some realizations and I truly do wonder if *she* was so fucked up because of someone in her life hurting her. Her dad? Someone in the church? I'm not sure which I think is *more* likely, but definitely both are possible. And I hate that for her—hate that for anyone—but..."

"But she hurt you and the reason behind the way she treated you isn't your burden to carry," I offered quietly, hoping the words were right.

"Yeah," Ben finally agreed. He took another breath. "Our sex life was sparse. She thought all sexual acts were dirty and anyone who got off on sex was the worst type of sinner. I think it would have been a lot worse if we'd spent more time together, but she didn't really want me around much—and after the beginning...when I figured out how terrible she was...I spent as much time away from her as possible. When she'd see me naked, she had complaints and nasty things to say. If I was hard, she made fun of me and told me I was dirty. Once, very early on, I asked her to touch my chest—my nipples—during sex and she used it against me pretty much until the day she died...talking about what a disgusting, dirty sinner I was." He paused, lost in thought. "I was this young, sheltered kid. I was a virgin on our wedding day. I'd barely learned about what I liked, I was messed up trying to hide the fact I liked guys. Sex is already messy and awkward—despite what movies, books, and porn would have us believe. And instead of learning with my wife, she belittled me and made me believe the things I fantasized about in bed would make me burn in hell." He shuddered. "It wasn't like I was thinking about seriously taboo stuff or anything super far out there. But she had definite opinions on what was *right* and *wrong* as far as sex. Kisses and spit were dirty. Semen was dirty. I had to wear a condom at all times and couldn't come inside her, even with the condom. She wore a tank top thing the whole time, her breasts were off limits for me to look at or touch. After I asked her to touch my nipples, she demanded I wear a shirt. The lights had to be off. There was *no* foreplay at all—the only way penetration actually happened was because I bought lubed condoms. She clearly didn't enjoy sex—she told me once she did it because it was her job as a Godly wife—and I quickly learned not to enjoy it either. At least not with her. I liked it fine in my fantasies and with myself."

"Wait, how in the world did she get pregnant if you couldn't come inside her?" I asked, truly curious, in addition to being in awe of what Ben had lived through. Not so much the sex he missed out on—sex was different for different people—but just the abuse he suffered. The amount of healing and growth he'd taken on and worked through was nearly miraculous.

"She paid for artificial insemination," Ben said. "I don't know that we would have had any problems getting pregnant, but she was so disgusted by the thought of me being inside her bare and coming in her that she opted to spend thousands to have a baby she didn't even want."

I pulled his arms tighter around me. "So, you jacked off in a cup and she got pregnant through medical technology—not because it was a need, but because of her screwed-up views of sex?"

Ben nodded. "Yeah. And maybe she was just disgusted by *me*. I don't know. But she didn't like sex. It wasn't even like she just didn't like penetration. I've read *a lot* about how sex is different for different people. I *do* think abuse in her past likely led to her feelings on sex. Combine that with the fact she was possibly asexual—probably sex-averse—and it made sense. I like to think I would have tried to be understanding—although, being forced into an arranged marriage with someone you barely knew and pretty much didn't like isn't a great foundation for accepting and understanding incompatibilities. But she wasn't one to *talk* about issues —she'd rather just belittle and judge and damn *me* to hell than talk about it or admit something was wrong—it was almost like she was angry with God for whatever had happened or just how she viewed sex even if there wasn't actually abuse in her past, and instead of being angry with God, she clung tighter to the church and put all the blame on me. I was her scapegoat."

"Have you dated since your separation and her death?"

Ben shook his head, one of his hands absently rubbing over the slight curve of my stomach. "Not really. I went out to dinner with a couple women, but there was absolutely no spark. There are quite a few attractive men in town, but they're mostly married. App hookups and dating aren't my thing."

I swallowed hard. "So, you're telling me you've never come inside a person during sex?" I asked, my voice thin and breathy as my cock sprung to life under the light blanket.

Ben tensed. "Is this where you figure out my baggage is too much and we promise to stay friends while never talking about this again?"

Chuckling, I shifted and moved my hands to his thighs. "You told your story. I'm willing to share mine if you'd like."

"Of course."

I cleared my throat. "We have this crazy connection, or at least, I feel like we do," I started. "And what you just told me makes me sure we found our way to each other for a reason."

Ben tensed and I huffed out a laugh.

"Don't worry, I'm not proposing marriage or anything." Trailing my fingers through the hair on his legs, I went on. "Remember when I said Scott and I weren't exactly compatible in bed?"

Ben nodded.

"Well, it had to do with me being a bottom with no desire to top and Scott being—well, back when we were together, it wasn't really a term used, but *now*, Scott would probably call himself a *side* as far as sex," I explained. "He didn't like giving or receiving anal sex."

"And that was a big deal for you?" Ben asked.

"Kinda...not really...clearly, we didn't break up because of it. We had so many good years together. But some of our biggest arguments stemmed from sex." I drew in a deep breath. "Overall, we kept each other and ourselves satisfied with a lot of great sexual stuff aside from anal—and he didn't mind using toys on me when the mood struck. Penetration isn't the be-all-end-all of sex, despite what society would have us believe."

"But?"

We both chuckled.

"But—" I hesitated.

"What?" Ben whispered in my ear. "You don't have to tell me anything, but I'm open to listening. I'm not going to judge you. I get it though, it was really hard for me to tell you about my sexual past."

I was quiet for a while and Ben spoke again.

"Would it help if I told you I *really* have a thing for my nipples being touched? I maybe haven't had sexual partners do it, but I play with them when I'm getting myself off—and it's definitely part of my fantasies."

I groaned and pressed a palm against my quickly thickening cock. "Scott didn't like to give anal and I've not been in a committed relationship since him—just casual sex between friends and *always* with condoms."

"That sounds safe and smart," Ben said. "But you want bare sex?"

His gruff words against my ear sent shivers down my spine.

"I want bare," I whispered before swallowing thickly. "And I have a fantasy about being bred. I want a guy to dump his load in my ass."

"Fuuuuck," Ben growled, his thick cock pressing hard against my lower back.

He reached for my dick, stroking it through the blanket.

"Does that turn you off? Bother you?" I asked.

"Fuck, no," he said.

"You like it?"

"She *never* let me be inside her without a condom. I've never come inside another person," he said. "Fuck, *yes*, I like it."

I cleared my throat and pushed up into Ben's touch. "While we're telling secrets," I said, "I like dirty talk. I like to be called names. Scott wasn't comfortable with it, but it totally gets me off."

Ben moved his hand under the blanket and took my

cock in hand. "Good to know, I'll keep that in mind...talk to you like the dirty little cock sucker you are," he murmured.

Oh.

My.

Fucking.

God.

TEN

Den

REGGIE'S COCK twitched in my hand and his sexy little groan went straight to my balls. This man...this man I'd come to think of as a friend and *more*...and now I found out some of his fantasies matched perfectly with mine.

Fuck.

That was heady stuff.

I gripped him tightly and sucked on his ear lobe before kissing his neck, biting gently, loving the way he writhed at my touch. "So, what I'm hearing this little slut say," I said, loving the way he trembled, his cock dripping pre-cum as I gave freedom to the words we both clearly wanted to hear, "is he wants to be my bottom bitch, Daddy's little cum hole?"

Reggie cried out, my words hitting something deep and needy inside him as he thrust his leaking cock into my fist.

"Answer me," I demanded, reaching to cup his balls, twisting gently in the same way I liked to play with my own. "Is that what you want? Wanna be Daddy's hole?

Let me use you like a toy? Just a hole for my load, you little cock whore?"

Reggie's release shuddered through him, exploding onto his stomach as he moaned, his hands gripping my thighs as he panted. "Fuck. Oh, fuck. Fuck, Ben."

"Mmmm," I hummed at his ear. "Love hearing you say my name when you come." He sniffled and I immediately worried I'd gone too far. "Was that okay? You were so good," I crooned.

Reggie wiped a tear from the corner of his eye as he turned to face me, yanking down the blanket to expose my throbbing cock and stretching out between my legs as if preparing for a feast. "*That* was like a fantasy come-to-life," he said, pressing his nose to where my sac pressed against the junction of my thigh. "Since we're making kinky dreams come true, let's see what I can do for you."

My cock dribbled pre-cum against my stomach. The fiery desire in Reggie's eyes spurred me on. He needed this as much as I did. Gripping the back of his head, my fingers tight in his hair, I took my cock in hand and smacked it against his cheek. "You greedy little cock sucker. Hungry for my cum?" I murmured. "Daddy's gonna face fuck you and choke you on my cum. Pour my load down your throat."

The sight of my pre-cum smearing against Reggie's pretty pink lips almost had me shooting on his face, but I squeezed hard, knowing how badly Reggie wanted this—how badly *I* wanted to unload in his mouth.

Reggie took my cock between his lips, sucked me deep, and I knew Heaven was real. Thrusting up, loving the tight heat of Reggie's throat, I tightened my hold on his hair. "Pretty little cock sucker," I growled. "Dirty little cock whore cum slut. Gonna make you choke on my cum."

Reggie hummed around my shaft, swallowing my cockhead, and teased his fingers over my nipple. Nearly sobbing in ecstasy, I hissed. "Yeah, play with Daddy's nipples, baby. Gonna make you suck my nipples and my cock when I finger your ass." Groaning when Reggie pinched one nipple and then the other, I continued, lost in the intoxicating fervor of my kinky fantasies come true. "Such a good boy, such a greedy little cock sucker, wanting all of Daddy's cum for yourself."

With one talented hand twisting my balls, his fingers playing with my sensitive nipples, and his throat opening around my throbbing cock, Reggie worked me to a frenzy. As my balls drew tight and my lower back tingled with hints of an impending release, my brain raged a battle.

Pull out, don't come in him, it's dirty and gross.

Give him what he wants. What you both want. Shoot your load, let him have your cum.

Reggie's pleading eyes caught mine, begging for me to give him my load.

"You want this? Want my cum?" I demanded.

A slight nod, a twist of my balls and my nipple, and I was lost. Even if I'd wanted to pull out, I wasn't sure I could. For the first time in my life, I orgasmed into a person, filling Reggie's waiting tongue and throat with my hot, thick load as I cried out and shook through release.

As if enough of my fantasies hadn't already come true for the night, Reggie let my spent dick slip from his mouth and shifted up my body. Bringing his lips to my nipples he dribbled the last of my cum over the tightly pebbled buds, swirling his tongue over the dusty-pink cum-covered skin before licking my load back into his mouth.

If I hadn't already come twice in one night, I probably would have shot another load right then and there. Instead, I urged Reggie farther up my body and brought our mouths together for a wet, sticky, messy kiss. I'd tasted my cum before, but the flavor of my release mixed with Reggie's unique taste had my senses on overload.

"Was that okay?" he murmured against my lips. Anxious worry creeping onto his face, threatening to burst our perfect little pleasure bubble.

Cupping the sides of his face in my hands, I made him look at me. "That was the most amazing, gorgeous, dream-come-true I never even thought could happen. You're so good," I paused at the tremor of delight traveling through him at the praise, "such a good boy for Daddy." Who knew dirty talk and a little praise would be something we both enjoyed so much? "I can't wait to have that pretty hole stretched open around my cock. Wanna hear you panting my name as I own your hole—that's all you'll be, my cum hole. Daddy's going to play with his toy and fill his pretty little cum slut with my load."

Reggie finally broke, sobbing, and pressed his forehead to mine. "Oh my god, Ben, I didn't know how badly I needed it. Needed *you*."

I wrapped my arms around him, bringing his head to rest on my chest, my hands caressing up and down his back, his ass, and back up to his shoulders. "I knew how badly I needed parts of it, but I never knew some of it would turn me on so much, and I never expected it would be with you."

"Are you disappointed?"

"Fuck, no. I love that we already had something sparking between us before we even discovered the sex part. I like you—I'm already obsessed with what we just did and what else we can do—and I want to keep it going." I gave his ass cheek a squeeze. "If you do."

"Yes. God, yes," Reggie said with a sigh. "But sleep first. We're old."

I laughed and slapped his ass. "Agreed. Shower?"

We made out in the shower, my nipples and dick highly sensitive after the heavy usage. Soaping Reggie's ass, I teased my fingers between the fleshy globes and pressed against his tight hole.

When Reggie whimpered, I grinned and nibbled at his ear. "Gonna love sliding into this pretty little hole. Love watching as you stretch open for Daddy's cock."

His knees buckled and he clung to my shoulders. "How the fuck are you so good at that?"

Chuckling, I shrugged, caressing his tight pucker. "I watch a lot of porn, but I think it's mostly just knowing how much you like it makes me want to do it and get you all worked up."

"Well, you're a beast and I never want you to stop."

We left the shower as the water ran cool, dried, and curled into each other in bed. With only a few hours until the sun would peek over the horizon, we needed rest before the day's adventures. The thought of spending the rest of the vacation adventuring around paradise with

Reggie during the day and exploring our fantasies at night had me smiling broadly against his damp hair as we drifted off to sleep.

A crack of thunder rattled the hut and woke me from the most amazing sleep of my life. Reggie cuddled in my arms, the warm afterglow of sex still clinging to our bodies, and something stirring in my heart had me smiling before I opened my eyes.

The room was dark as a storm raged outside.

Reggie shifted in my arms and mumbled something about one more hour.

I kissed his ear and whispered, "Sleep. We're not going anywhere in the rain."

When I rolled out of bed, Reggie turned to his side, hiding his head under the pillow.

Checking my phone, I realized with a start that it wasn't dark because it was early, it was dark because of the storm. My clock read just after noon. Reggie and I had slept a full eight hours, the dreary skies keeping the sun from waking us. Glancing outside, I checked the radar on my weather app. We were in for an all-day rain with occasional storms. The meteorologist's blog suggested movies in bed for the day. Movies? Maybe not. In bed? Yeah, Reggie and I could handle that.

After a quick trip to the bathroom to freshen up a bit, I started the water for tea. While the kettle heated, I scrolled through the island's list of places that would deliver. I hated to make a person get out in the mess of rain, but we had no food in the hut aside from a few snacks. If Reggie and I got up to all the fun my brain and dick were imagining, we were going to need fuel.

When the text from Jason popped up on my screen, I had a sudden urge to blush and hide my phone as if the kid could see the dirty thoughts I was having about his dad.

Shit.

The kids.

How would they handle Reggie and me being together?

Did they need to know?

Would it last beyond paradise?

What if we went through the drama of telling them, only to have the spark die out? Was it worth it?

But if they found out somehow and knew we'd been hiding it...

I huffed out a sigh and ran a hand over my face as the kettle clicked off, the thought of losing whatever had bloomed between Reggie and me making me as dreary as the day outside.

> Jason: We ordered a bunch of food and groceries for the day. When you hear a knock at your door, open it. I told them to leave it at the door, but I don't want it to get wet.

Just as I clicked to type a reply, a knock sounded at the door. I opened it to find two bags of groceries and three delivery bags, all in a large tote covered in a poncho-like thing. I grabbed the delivery and brought it inside, placing it on the table, before sending a *thank you* back to Jason.

Jason: Where's Dad?

Me: Still asleep.

Shit.

How would I explain Reggie still sleeping at almost one in the afternoon?

Jason: Is he sick? What's wrong?

Me: We were up late. Didn't go to sleep until almost sunrise. Slept late.

That didn't sound suspicious, right? I mean, it wasn't like I told the kid I'd kissed his dad, got off with him, shared stories from our pasts, and then spent the rest of the night playing out kinky fantasies.

Jason: That's not like him, you sure he's
not sick?

As I started to reply, Reggie chuckled.

I turned to see him rubbing sleep from his eyes as he
looked at the group text on his phone.

Reggie: I'm awake now since my phone
was blowing up. Thanks for the
groceries. You guys just hanging out in
your hut today?

He glanced up at me, his face awash with the glow of his
phone screen. A soft smile and hungry eyes told me
Reggie felt as good as I did about last night. I had a
feeling neither of us were going to be upset about a day
stuck in the hut.

Jason: Yeah. Just gonna relax ;) Matt
and Tara may come over later.

I shuddered and Reggie laughed.

"What?" I groused. "I don't need to think about what
your son plans on doing to my baby girl."

"He said *relax*," Reggie teased. "What's wrong with *relax*?"

I threw a scowl over my shoulder. "You know exactly what that winky face meant. He's talking about the type of relaxing that may make us grandfathers before we're fifty."

Reggie grinned. "You know the kids have no plans to have kids right away."

"Not the point," I growled.

"How about we let them have their fun and we can *relax* in our own way," Reggie asked, biting his lip as he watched me.

I shrugged. "Go." I gestured toward the bathroom. "Tea is almost ready and I'll unload the food."

Once Reggie had taken care of a quick morning routine, he lit four candles around the room. "It's nice the resort provides candles. I'm guessing dark, stormy days aren't all that unusual, even on a tropical island," he chattered.

The hut took on a cozy atmosphere as the waves pounded, the rain poured, and the candles cast a soft glow.

I put the few things that needed to be kept cold in the little fridge, arranged the other food and snacks on the small countertop, and dug into the delivery bags. "We've got French toast, bagels, breakfast sandwiches, fruit, yogurt..." I paused and chuckled, "and what looks like an entire pizza packed into take-out containers. What do you want?"

Reggie grinned. "Jason knows I love cold pizza for breakfast."

"Mmmm, same." My stomach rumbled in time to the rolling thunder as one storm passed and another built.

"But the pizza will be fine at lunch," Reggie said. "Well, dinner, I guess. Let's do the breakfast type stuff. We'll have a fashionably late brunch."

I looked out the door of the hut. "The patio is dry. Wanna eat out there? Light the heaters, start a fire in the pit, stuff our faces to the sound of the rain before another storm rolls in?"

Reggie's eyes danced. "That sounds amazing. Didn't realize you're such a romantic," he teased.

"I'm good for more than just dull and uncultured," I teased back.

Reggie rolled his eyes. "You do know I was completely wrong about that and I'm sorry, right?"

Wrapping an arm around his waist and pulling him close, I bent my head to take his mouth in mine. After a long, sensual kiss that had me wondering if we could just crawl right back into bed, I finally dragged my lips away. "I know. And I was wrong about you being overly dramatic and too much."

He huffed a laugh. "No, no, you weren't. I am those things. I'm also a bundle of worry and nerves and constantly on the go."

I cocked my head. "I noticed that in the beginning, but not so much now."

His cheeks pinked slightly in the dim light. "Yeah, that's been kinda weird. Usually trips make my anxiety sky rocket—and this one did in the beginning, almost worse than any other I've been on—but once I got settled in here, my nerves eased more than ever." Reggie cleared his throat. "I'm gonna pull out some of the drama here, but it feels like being around you calms me. Not like I'm going to give up therapy or yoga or medication—and I'll never be completely anxiety-free, none of us are—but *this*," he gestured between us, "this has given me something else to focus on. Like I don't need the stimulation of the worry and nerves because you're here."

I raised a brow and grinned. "So, I'm just a distraction, huh?"

A look of panic crossed his face. "No, not that at all. God, I didn't mean it like that. And it's not like I expect you to continue this just because I said it helps me. Shit, that's a lot of pressure. You can end this any time. I'm not your responsibility and you don't have—"

Gripping his chin and forcing his eyes up to mine, I interrupted his spiral. "Reggie, breathe. I was joking. I'm glad you feel better around me. I feel better around you too." His words played back through my head. "Do you want me to end this?" The thought soured my stomach. We'd just found each other—all the better because neither of us had been really *looking*—I wasn't ready for it to end. But maybe I was more of a fling for him than he was for me.

"God, no. But I don't want to be clingy. You said you weren't looking for anything—"

"I said I wasn't looking because I'd know if something *right* came along," I corrected. "I have a lifetime of experience with *wrong*, so I trust my heart to know when something is right." Clearing my throat, I decided it was as good a time as any to clear the air. "I want to see where this goes. Period. No more talk about ending it—unless we both decide down the road that things just aren't working."

"And when we get back home?"

I shook my head. "No need to borrow trouble beyond paradise. We've got plenty of time." Kissing his sweet lips again, I smiled and nuzzled my nose against his. "Now, get the patio set up while I make breakfast." Maybe I was avoiding, the proverbial ostrich with my head in the sand, but it didn't make sense to get worked up over something that hadn't happened yet.

Fifteen minutes later, I carried a tray of food and drinks outside to our own little covered paradise. A fire flickered in the pit, the ocean air mixed with the heater's warmth, and soft music played from Reggie's speaker.

"This is damn cozy," I said once we'd filled our plates with a variety of food from the tray. "I need a spot like this back home."

"It's nice," Reggie murmured. "Back home, the winter months would make it useless."

"Nah," I said around a bite of French toast. "We can do an outside one and an inside one. I've already got a nice patio, but I want to cozy it up a bit. And I'm thinking I'll add a little book nook type cozy spot inside by my picture window. Cushions and pillows, blankets and built-in speakers. It's near a fireplace, so it would be the perfect winter cuddle spot. Just need to replace the window to make sure it's well insulated."

Reggie cocked his head as he bit into a bagel. "Is the house you're in now the one you and Lariah shared?"

I shuddered. "No, I couldn't do it. Too many bad memories. My first shop was in the garage of that house and I basically lived there. But I moved myself and my business a while back. I love the shop and the house. The house keeps me busy with little odds and ends, it's older, but it has a lot of character." Frowning, I tried to think if I knew where Reggie lived. "I guess I've only ever seen you at Jason's or Megan's place since they got together. Do you have a house in town?"

He shook his head. "No, after Scott died, I sold the house and moved into an apartment. I miss house-living in some ways, but it's nice to have someone else taking care of the up-keep and repairs."

"I wonder if the kids will miss their apartments now that they're moving into a house," I mused.

"I'm sure they'll find home-ownership has pros and cons," Reggie said, grinning around a bite of yogurt.

"What do you want to do today?" I asked as we worked our way through breakfast.

"You want the socially appropriate answer or the actual real answer?" Reggie asked, his eyes locked on mine as a grin teased his lips.

"Well, now you've got me curious, how 'bout both?"

How were things so damn easy with him? When I'd started to realize my life was far from normal—and then, when I'd woken up to the fact I *had* to get myself and Megan away from the toxicity—I'd taken comfort in knowing not *all* relationships were as painful and stifling as the ones I'd known with my parents and wife.

But I'd never once met someone who was as easy to be around as Reggie. We'd been casual acquaintances for a while thanks to the kids getting together, but it wasn't as if I'd known much about the man outside of my preconceived notions. So, why did such a short amount of time spent with him leave me feeling like we'd known each other a lifetime?

"Socially appropriate," Reggie began, schooling his features and sitting up straight. "Since we're stuck inside all day, we should watch some movies and maybe read a little. I *do* have some books I said I'd take time to read while on this vacation."

Standing, I grabbed his hand and yanked him up until we were chest-to-chest. Smiling at his squawk, I lowered us down to the outdoor couch, me on my back, my hands skimming over his ass and sneaking up his shirt to scratch his back. "Books? You mean your romance novels?"

"Shhhh," Reggie said, glancing around as if worried he'd be scandalized. "When being socially appropriate, one doesn't discuss such things as *romance* novels."

"Why's that?" I asked with a chuckle.

"One is to be concerned with being *proper* and reading *only* texts that stimulate the brain," Reggie said, really playing it up. "It is not *proper* to read about people falling in love—rots the mind. If truly proper people have to be miserable as they bathe in their hateful judgment, then *all* should be required to do the same." Somewhere along the line, he'd picked up an accent of sorts, although, I couldn't quite place it.

"Falling in *love*?" I asked, pretending to be horrified.

Reggie pressed a finger to my lips. "Shhhhh, we mustn't speak of it. Happily ever afters bring the miserable, proper folks to their knees. If they can't be happy, no one should be happy." He glanced around before whispering, "And some of the romance novels even have *s-e-x* in them."

I gasped, having fun playing along as his body pressed down on mine. "No! Not..." I pretended to make sure no one was around. "S-e-x? Very improper, indeed."

Reggie bit the corner of his lip. "Indeed," he answered with a nod. "Throw in the fact that *my* romance novels are mostly *gay* couples wrapped up in sex and love, and the *proper* society likely wouldn't survive it."

Caught up in the moment, loving the easy fun and the warmth between our bodies, I cupped the back of his head and pulled him in for a long, leisurely kiss. When we finally broke apart, I asked, "And the real answer?"

Reggie blinked rapidly, pulling himself out of our pleasure haze. "Huh? Oh, right." He caught his bottom lip between his teeth. "We're stuck inside on a rainy day. I say we clean up our mess, take a little time to prep, and then spend the rest of the day in bed."

"Mmmm, a nap *does* sound good," I teased, doing my best to hold back a laugh. "Not sure I could sleep *all* day, but there's just something about a nap on a rainy day."

"Perhaps I'm not making myself clear," Reggie said, his hands cupping my face. "I want to repeat last night, but more. Want you to stretch me open. Want you to fuck me."

The air crackled with sexual tension, but there was more than just sex between us. So much more.

I wasn't sure which was scarier, the thought of fucking this man and leaving it all on the island.

Or the thought of what was building between us being the first day of the rest of our lives.

Together.

Both were terrifying.

But I had a gut-deep sense that only one of the options would bring me true happiness and fulfill me in ways I'd never dreamed possible.

For the longest time, I'd not even known *more* was possible for me.

Then Reggie came along.

And a world of possibilities opened up.

But the only possibility my heart and body longed for was *him*.

"Ben?" Reggie asked, uncertainty etched on his face.

"Romance novels can wait—proper people be damned—I think I have an all-day-in-bed date to attend." I kissed him long and slow before pulling away with a groan. Slapping his ass, I said, "Go, take care of whatever you need to." I knew bottoming wasn't something that just miraculously happened without a little bit of forethought. "I'll clean up."

Reggie headed toward the bathroom, but stopped and cleared his throat. "Um, before things get too heated and we're thinking with the wrong heads," he said.

I raised a brow.

"I've been tested three times in the past year and have only ever used condoms with the few casual partners I've had. And obviously penetrative sex wasn't a thing with Scott. I'm negative." He bit his lip. "As much as it's fun to talk about going bare and breeding and all that, we both have to be sure we're comfortable with it.

I'd never want to put you in a position where you don't feel safe."

Smiling, I moved across the little room and kissed him, his concern making me like him that much more. "I haven't had a sexual partner aside from myself since long before Lariah died. An early session with Bruce brought up an unspoken suspicion I had that maybe Lariah was sleeping with others aside from me. She'd never allowed sex without a condom, but I made sure to get tested after each encounter. When we eventually stopped having sex altogether, I still made sure to have tests done just to be sure."

"So, we're good with going without?" Reggie asked, his words breathy and his pupils blown.

"I'm on board." Cupping his face and nuzzling my nose against his, I went on. "As long as whatever this is stays just between us unless we have a conversation about it changing. I'm good going bare with *you*, not anyone else at this point."

Reggie nodded, closing his eyes and pressing his cheek into my hand. "Yeah, same." Just as he started to turn toward the bathroom, he stopped. "And um, just so you know, I don't need the kinky sex all the time. I like the good ol' fashioned sweet and steamy stuff too."

Gripping his ass and rocking our hips together, I smiled. "Noted. And for the record, I'm on board with sweet and steamy too."

Reggie pulled away and headed toward the bathroom, leaving me to once again wonder just how I'd gotten so lucky and how things were so breezily easy with him.

After taking care of our brunch mess, I checked some emails on my shop account, replied to a couple customers regarding their orders and possible project quotes, and adjusted my schedule to meet the needs of a few jobs I needed to finish before I could start anything new. Even though I was loving every second of the island getaway—I wondered for a moment what the trip would have been like if Reggie and I hadn't struck up a friendship, would I still be grousing around and wishing I was in Alaska?—I was still a small business owner and I had responsibilities to take care of.

When Reggie emerged from the steamy bathroom wrapped in a towel, all of my focus moved to him. Closing my laptop, I packed it away and moved to pull him close. "Don't get dressed. I'm going to take the world's quickest shower."

Reggie moaned into my mouth, greedy for my kisses, before answering with a whimpery *okay*.

True to my word, I took very little time cleaning up and walked out of the bathroom to a storm-darkened room painted in the golden-glow of candlelight.

And a very naked Reggie sipping tea as he leaned against the patio door and stared out at the storm.

"Should we add exhibitionist to your breeding kink?" I asked gruffly as I bent to kiss his neck, my hand sliding around to palm his dick.

"Mmmmm," Reggie moaned, "maybe. But it's more the *chance* of being watched than the actual act of being watched."

"Anything else?"

"How do you feel about toys?" Reggie asked.

A low rumble erupted from my chest.

"I take that as a yes?" A grin teased at Reggie's words.

"Toys were a dirty sin, of course. I've used a few on myself, but I'm not above the good ol' hand and fingers getting the job done. You like them?" I stroked his cock, thumbing over the leaking slit as I buried my nose in his fresh, clean hair.

"Sometimes fingers just don't get the job done as well as a thick dildo when you're dying for that stretch and burn," Reggie said.

"Fuck," I growled. "I didn't pack any toys, but I can give you the stretch and burn."

He thrust into my hand with a curse.

"Wanna get you off right here where anyone could see you come in my hand," I murmured at his ear.

Reggie must have liked the idea because he shivered and moaned, thrusting harder in my fist.

"Mmmm, my little cock whore likes the idea of being watched. You wanna get off knowing absolutely anyone who happens by could see? What would they think to see a dirty little cum slut being jerked off and coming in the rain?" The words gave me power. Reggie's whimpers spurred me on. My rock-hard cock pressed between his ass cheeks, begging to slide into his tight heat.

Taking the mug from his hand, I wildly shoved it toward the table in hopes it didn't spill. "Lift your hands up and spread your legs," I demanded. A part of me that had never had the chance to spark to life with Lariah— and maybe not with *any* woman, sex with a man had a completely different vibe, or at least it did with Reggie— took over as thunder rolled in time with the ocean waves.

"Want you spread out like the greedy little hole you are, out in the open for anyone to see."

The gentle rain pounded the tin roof of the hut as the warm breeze blew damp air against our bare skin. A desperate sound escaped Reggie as he reached over his head to grip the door frame, spreading his legs wide, his head thrown back in ecstasy. With my throbbing shaft pressed against his hole, I jerked him slow and steady in time with his thrusts. Adding a twist on each up stroke, just the way I liked to get myself off, I trailed my other hand down his chest and abdomen, moving to cup his balls. They were drawn tight, letting me know Reggie was about to blow. "That's it, my greedy little whore, come for Daddy." Each word, each whimper from Reggie, each shudder my words sent through him, worked to unknot something deep inside me. Years of being told I was dirty and depraved for daring to like sex unraveled as I worked Reggie into a frenzy. The words gave me freedom to be who I was, to like what I liked, to love who I loved.

My heart catching in my chest at the thought of feeling that way for Reggie, I jacked him harder, loving the way he cried out. "Come for me, dirty boy. Let me hear you."

Reggie's arms dropped, his hands over his head, and gripped tightly behind my neck as his orgasm tore through him. He unloaded long, thick ropes of cum onto the patio and my brain fought to break through the haze long enough to think about making sure we cleaned that up later.

When his shuddering stopped, I turned him around

and pulled him close, capturing his mouth as I smeared my cum-covered fingers around his tight pucker. "Gonna work you open with my tongue and come in this pretty little hole," I promised. When Reggie moaned into my mouth, I chuckled. "Is that what you want? Want Daddy's cum filling you up?"

"Fuck, yes," Reggie said. "Let me suck you first." He pushed me down onto the mattress. Spreading my legs, he nuzzled his nose into my pubes. "Love this cock," he murmured before taking me deep to the back of his throat.

Leaning back on my hands, I enjoyed the wet heat of his mouth. When his head continued to bob as both hands moved to tease my nipples, I groaned. My balls drew up tight and I pulled out of his mouth. "Don't want to come that way," I said. I'd always known my nipples were sensitive, but the combination of Reggie's mouth on my cock and his fingers playing with the tight buds proved to be almost more than I could handle. "Maybe another time, but I wanna come in your ass."

Reggie licked his lips, savoring the pre-cum I'd given him and stood, his cock already coming back to life.

"That's an impressive refractory," I teased.

"Been a long time, I'm as horny as a teen." He squeezed his cock as a blush painted his cheeks.

"On your stomach," I demanded, my own cock twitching in anticipation. Sex had never been something I got to control. Sex had never been enjoyable. Sex had never involved such strong feelings of attraction and connection. Now, sex was all of that and more. My head buzzed and I fought to ground myself, wanting to savor every moment.

Moving between Reggie's legs, I sank to my belly and placed my hands on the full, round globes of his ass. Spreading his cheeks apart, I buried my face in his ass and pressed my tongue against his hole.

Reggie cried out, humping into the mattress. "Fuck, Ben."

"You good?" I asked.

"Yeah."

Licking and sucking, swirling my tongue, eating ass for the first time in my life and loving every second of it, I worked him open. I teased and thrust my tongue, imagining what I'd like if Reggie were to rim me.

"Oh god," Reggie cried out. "Please."

"Please what?"

"Ben, fuck. I wanna feel you inside me."

Suddenly worried I had no clue how to stretch him properly, I pulled back. "Did you bring any toys?"

"We don't have to—"

"Wanna make sure I prep you right," I said.

"You sure?" Reggie asked. "We can stop if you—"

"Reg, I'm about to bust a nut I want inside you so bad. I've never done this before, wanna make sure I don't hurt you. Figured a dildo might be better to stretch you than my fingers. That's all," I said, hoping to ease his worries.

"That black bag, side pocket. Wrapped in a washcloth."

When my search provided a dildo just about the size and color of my own dick, I couldn't help but chuckle.

"Bet the screeners have seen a lot worse, but they probably had a laugh at this." Grabbing a bottle of lube at the same time, I made my way back to the bed. "I'd love to hear some of their stories."

Reggie chuckled as he watched me approach. "Luckily, they didn't opt to search. I always have this fear of them opening my bag and waving silicone cocks around."

"What's most comfortable for you?" I asked, forgetting the airport security discussion the moment I joined him on the bed.

Reggie rolled to his back, his recovered cock smearing another round of pre-cum on his stomach.

Coating the dildo and his hole with lube, I stretched out beside him and pressed the silicone head to his tight pucker. "Tell me what to do," I whispered, kissing the side of his mouth. "Tell me to stop if it's too much."

Reggie feathered his lips over my cheek. "Just go slow, been a while. And kiss me."

Our mouths mated, hot and wet, slick tongues dancing as I pushed the toy ever so slowly into his body. Reggie whimpered when the dildo breached the tight ring of muscle and I paused as his hole stretched and adjusted. "You good?"

He nodded and hissed a *yesss*, spreading his legs as his mouth met mine again. We kissed for several moments as I worked the dildo in and out of his hole. When Reggie's fingers skimmed over my nipples, I thrust my cock against his leg.

"Love playing with your nipples, so sensitive," Reggie

said, bringing his head up to take a pebbled nipple into his mouth.

"Fuuuuck," I groaned, the flick of his tongue against my sensitive flesh going straight to my balls.

"Wanna try to get you off with just my fingers in your ass and my tongue on your nipples someday," Reggie said, sucking hard enough to make me hiss.

"Fuck, yeah," I growled.

"I might be a bottom, but that doesn't mean I can't get into some ass and nipple play with the right guy," Reggie said. "But until then, I'm gonna need you to get that gorgeous cock in my hole."

"I've read about bossy bottoms," I teased, propping myself up to watch the flesh-colored silicone shaft slide in and out, Reggie's ring stretched open. Slowly easing the toy from his body, I tossed it to the side and reached for the lube to coat my cock. Moving between Reggie's legs, I pressed the leaking head of my cock to his hole. He took me in easily, both of us groaning as my thick cock slid into his tight heat.

Part of me begged to call him names, talk dirty, go at it hard and fast, but my heart caught in my chest when Reggie's eyes met mine.

This was so different.

So right.

This was *real* and my heart demanded a change from the plan.

Watching my cock slide in and out of his ass for a moment, I shifted to bring us chest-to-chest. Cupping Reggie's face, every positive sensation in the world gathering at the point where we'd become one, I whispered, "Hi" and nuzzled my nose against his.

Reggie's voice shook when he whispered "Hi" back to me, his eyes shining brightly as I fucked in and out of his body, every single thing I felt for him pouring from me with each thrust, each word, each kiss.

We had time for the dirty talk.

Time for kink.

It could wait.

At that very moment, I needed to make love to Reggie in a way I'd never once been able to make love to my wife. Slowly, intimately, savoring every touch, every whimper, every white-hot clench of his body around me.

This was what I'd longed for.

The connection, the heat, the acceptance.

The love.

I knew it was too soon.

Too much.

Absolutely crazy.

But I'd lived my whole life knowing exactly what love *wasn't*, so it was abundantly clear to me what I felt for Reggie was the real thing.

Just like the dirty talk and kinky shit, the declaration could wait.

But I knew, in that moment, Reggie was the other half to my whole.

My person.

My future.

If he'd have me.

Reggie moaned as I thrust deep, his legs wrapping around my waist and his lips clinging to mine.

Lost in his body, drunk on the sensations of our joining, hypnotized by the sounds washing over us—ocean waves, gentle rain, sweaty flesh—I buried my face in Reggie's neck and rocked into him over and over.

He gripped my ass and cried out as I hit his prostate again and again. "Oh god, Ben, fuck. Give it to me."

"What do you want?" I asked, my balls drawing tight at the thought of spilling my load into someone for the first time in my life.

"Your cum," Reggie sobbed, "give me your cum."

Any semblance of control I'd been pretending to have disappeared as quickly as the lightning. I pressed up onto my hands and fucked into him in a deep, slow rhythm as Reggie stroked his leaking cock.

When he shuddered, spurts of cum splattering his stomach and his ass clenching tightly around my shaft, I couldn't hold off any longer. Grunting on a final hard thrust, I held myself deep as my orgasm roared through me. Each pulse of my cock painting my load deep in Reggie's hole as he whimpered and babbled nonsense under me.

As we came down from our high, I dropped to press our chests together and hold him tightly in my arms. Cuddling after sex was something I'd always wanted but never experienced. Reggie's sniffle had me studying his face in concern. "You okay? Shit, was it bad?"

His watery laugh sent a tear leaking from the corner of his eye. "No, you big dope, it was amazing. Honestly, I've never had sex that good."

I raised a brow.

"Yeah, even with Scott. I'm feeling a bit guilty for

even thinking it. What he and I shared was good, comfortable, easy and full of love. But it was different than what we just did."

"You're allowed to feel however you feel. It was definitely the best I've ever had. Going bare *and* coming inside you was amazing. Overwhelming."

Reggie moaned and tightened his ass around me. "Fuck, yeah, so good."

"Sorry we didn't get to the dirty talk," I mumbled against his neck, my whole body limp and relaxed. My spent cock slipped from Reggie's ass and we both groaned.

"Told you, I don't always need that. I went decades without it, it's not something I *have* to have. It's just fun and gets me off. We have time."

"Two weeks in paradise," I murmured. "I think we'll spend the rest of our trip making the best of our time."

Reggie chuckled. "Pretty sure we can come up with something."

I wanted to talk about the time we'd have together when we got home, but I wondered if it was too much, too soon. We'd both indicated we wanted whatever this was to continue when we got home, but was it stupid to think we could actually pull it off?

With emotions running high, maybe it was best to focus on the time we had left on the island and not borrow trouble by worrying about what we'd be when we got back home.

ELEVEN

Reggie

AFTER THE BEST sex of my life, Ben wrapped me in his arms and we slept like the dead as the elements outside our cozy little hut cycled through gentle rain, thunderstorms, and back to a soft downpour.

I came awake slowly sometime later, reveling in the tropical breeze blowing through the patio door, the soft floral scent of the island mixed with the sandalwood of the candles, and the warm strength of the man holding me close.

Scott had been my very best friend and we'd been happy. I didn't regret a single moment I'd spent with him. We had a lifetime of good memories and I missed him every day. Most importantly, I knew he'd be so damn happy to know I'd found someone to make my life whole again.

Shit, that's heavy. Is Ben even in the market for forever?

I thought back to the bits and pieces of conversation we'd had. Ben straight-up said he wanted to see where things could go between us, but when I brought up what things would be like back home, he'd pushed the question away by saying there was no need to borrow trouble beyond paradise.

Did that mean Ben thought a relationship with me would be trouble? Was he expecting we'd go back to our old lives and pretend our two weeks in paradise never happened? Was Ben worried about the kids finding out? People around town? Maybe his business suffering? Would he expect us to keep things under wraps?

Something tugged in my chest. I wasn't sure I could do that. I wasn't at a point in my life where I wanted to hide. Losing Scott had shown me the importance of living each day to the fullest—or at least to the best of my ability. My anxiety wouldn't allow for a secret relationship with a man I'd fallen head-over-heels with.

Truth-be-told, my heart already beat a rhythm that sounded very much like *forever* in regards to what Ben and I had. But I had to be honest with myself, perhaps Ben's past hurts were so much that forever wasn't something he was capable of.

The press of Ben's hot shaft between my ass cheeks pulled me from the spiral of *what ifs* and brought me crash landing to the present. Smack dab back in the arms of the very real man rocking his hips against my backside and kissing my neck.

"Are you sore?" Ben asked, his lips hot against my skin.

"No, you took good care of me."

"Fuck," he growled. "Why is that so hot?"

I pressed my ass into his hips. "You have something in mind?"

"Thought my little cum slut might want another load," he said, his gravely words going straight to my balls. "Wanna slide into my sweet little cock whore, feel his hole slick with my cum, and breed his ass until he can't take anymore."

I whimpered, my cock plumping and my ass clenching as he spoke. "Fuck, Ben."

"You want this cock? Wanna feel my bare dick in your greedy little hole?"

"God, yes, please," I begged.

"What else do you want?" Ben's lips moved gently against my ear as he pressed his hard length between my ass cheeks.

"Your cum, want it dripping from my hole. Wanna feel you unload deep inside me again."

Ben took hold of his cock and pressed the leaking head against my still-slick hole. Lifting my leg for better access, easing his way into the tight muscle, he groaned when I opened for him, taking him deep inside.

"Fuck, Reggie," Ben said, his words like a prayer. "Already wet with my cum and begging for more like the cum hole you are."

Every word he spoke lit a fire deep in my belly and I cried out when Ben bottomed out, his balls pressed against me. "Give it to me. Please. Breed me," I sobbed, the slick friction of Ben's cock pumping deep into my hole sending lava through my veins.

"Beg for it, you dirty little bottom-boy. Beg for Daddy's cock."

My body burned with sensations, sensory overload, and I gripped Ben's hand, leading it to my dripping cock. "Please, Ben, breed me. Fill me up."

"Say it, tell me what you want," Ben commanded.

"Fuck me," I panted. "Fill me with your babies."

Ben groaned, thrusting into me hard and fast as he stroked my cock. "Come for me, Reg, let me feel that tight little hole around my fat cock."

His words hit hard just as his cockhead brushed over my prostate and I cried out, my orgasm erupting over Ben's fist. With a roar, he gripped my hip with his sticky, slick hand and slammed into me. Unleashing his hot load deep in my ass, Ben buried his face in my neck, grunting with each pulse of his cock in my tight channel.

"Holy shit," he mumbled when we both finally caught our breaths. "That was..."

"Intense? Amazing? Earth-shattering?" I murmured, kissing the inner wrist of the arm he had wrapped around me.

"All of the above," Ben answered, his voice holding a grin and exhaustion. "Who knew the sheltered little boy from the corrupt Bible-thumping family of bigots would turn out to be such a fan of dirty talk?" he asked, awe and satisfaction lacing his words.

"And be so damn good at it," I answered on a sigh. "Have you always liked talking dirty and just didn't get a chance?"

"I can't say I've always liked it, never really had a chance to try it. I mean," Ben went on, "I've heard it in porn and read articles about adding it to your sex life, but I wasn't calling myself names when I jacked off at home all these years." The huff of laughter was relieved more than self-deprecating. "And then you said you liked it and everything kinda clicked."

"Well, you're amazing and I love it. Keep up the good work," I teased.

Ben chuckled. "Only took years of suppressing the real me, years of being made to feel shame about things as natural as attraction and sex. Talking to you like that —*especially* because you like it so much—is freeing in a way. Like my chance to claim who I really am—without fear and shame."

"I'm sorry you had to go through that," I started.

"Me too," Ben interrupted. "It was hell, but talking to Bruce has taught me that I can't change the past, I can only take my experiences and use them to better my future."

I sighed as he slipped from my body and his cum-covered cock pressing against my inner thigh. "Therapy is good for people. Kinda wish it was a requirement. I mean, I'm sure there are shitty therapists, and maybe some people don't *need* it as much as others, but I think the world would be so much better if everyone had better access to improving their mental and emotional health."

"Gotta be willing to put in the effort," Ben said. "But I agree."

"I'm assuming things, but your family didn't see therapy as a good thing?"

Ben full-on laughed before bringing his lips to my temple. "Understatement. The church encouraged pre-marital counseling for young couples planning to get married, and marriage counseling for those already wed, but it was all Bible-based." He snorted. "Or it was all based on the corrupt interpretation of the Bible by men in the church who called themselves counselors. When we went before we got married—it was required—it was just a bunch of serve your husband, serve God, serve the church, serve the kingdom we'll one day inherit. So much shit. But Lariah ate it up." He breathed deeply, nuzzling his nose into my hair as his hand caressed over my belly. "Before I'd left the church and Lariah, back when our parents were still alive and helping with all the corruption, I overhead a counseling session." Ben paused, a tension in his words. "It was one of the many moments that finally culminated in me leaving and figuring myself out, but the woman—she was there by herself, without her husband—was sobbing about how he hurt her." His body tightened with anger. "The fucking counselor was one of the deacons in the church. He told her that she was a sinner and the only way to ensure her place in Heaven was to serve God by serving her husband. She left crying—I don't know what happened to her, I don't think I ever saw her at church again—and the counselor laughed as she ran out of the building. When he saw me, he cupped his crotch and said something like, 'If Allen doesn't rip her open tonight, she can come serve *this* god.'"

"That is *vile*," I said. "I hope she got away and started a new life for herself."

Ben hummed against my shoulder. "It's more likely she was beaten to death and the church covered it up. Paul, the counselor, would have immediately told Allen, her husband. Hell," a shaky breath whooshed from him, "they probably both had a go at her as punishment before they killed her. God, sorry, nothing like being a total downer. I just sometimes think there's more I could be doing to fight the evil in that church."

"Hey," I said, my hand squeezing his. "You're one person. If you decide to fight, I'd support you. But going up against them individually would be *a lot*, especially when you suffered half of your life at the hand of the church. You have a story to tell and it might help others, but you have to save yourself first before you can save them. And I don't think you should do it alone. Didn't you say you question the way Lariah's parents died? The church—at least *that* one—is dangerous. And probably a lot more powerful than we can even imagine. Just the little bit of shit you've told me is stuff documentaries are made of."

Ben sighed. "Yeah, I just can't help but feel guilty that I got out and there are so many still stuck." He huffed a bitter laugh. "And most of them don't even realize they're stuck because they're brainwashed."

We fell silent for a while, the euphoria of sex, the heavy conversation, and the tropical rainstorm weighing over us.

"You wanna shower? Probably need to switch these sheets," I said. "We could get some food and read on the patio."

By the time night rolled around, Ben and I had enjoyed both lunch and dinner on the patio, spent time reading—he was hooked on a romance novel I'd let him borrow—took another nap, and made cocktails to sip by the fire.

The rain continued, but it had lessened to just a soft sprinkle. Comfy-cozy under Ben's arm, I sipped whatever tropical concoction he'd mixed up.

"Whatcha thinkin?" Ben asked, his words warm and easy.

"Just that I don't think my anxiety will ever go away, but stepping away from home and work—just taking a moment to breathe and enjoy—has helped me wind down so much."

"Think you could do that back home?" Ben asked. "Force yourself to take a breather, even if it's not in paradise?"

"Yeah," I sighed. "I'd miss the tropical island," I teased, "but I could require myself to build in breathers. Keep up the therapy, spend a little more time in yoga, allow myself to let others take care of things. I'm not the only one at work who can do things right—even though my pride likes to make me think so."

"That's good. You deserve breaks. You definitely seem more relaxed now than I've ever seen you."

I scoffed. "That may be because you've fucked me within an inch of my life."

Ben chuckled.

We fell silent, sipping our drinks as the ever-present ocean serenaded us.

A knock sounded at the front door to the hut. Moments later, Jason called from the side yard as he approached the patio, "Dad? Ben?"

Ben froze and then quickly stood, nearly toppling me to the ground. "Out here," he called, stepping to the side of the patio and raising a drink in greeting.

My son was all smiles when he stepped onto the patio. Married life on an island was clearly doing him well. He glanced between Ben and me, his eyes narrowing.

Could he tell we'd been fucking each other's brains out all day? Did Jason know I was a total slut for dirty talk? How would he feel about his dad's breeding kink? Pretty sure no child—no matter their age—wanted to think about their father-in-law barebacking their dad.

A snort of laugher bubbled from deep inside. The cocktail was definitely getting to me.

Ben shot me a look, but I couldn't read his expression. He'd basically dropped me like a hot potato the second we heard Jason at the door. Was this how it would be back home? Secret rendezvous filled with glorious, steamy, kinky sex, but the moment the kids or anyone else was in the picture, we were just two guys stuck together because our kids got married?

"Just wanted to let you know, our nighttime island tour is still on," Jason said. "They called to say the rain was light enough and the main part of the storm has moved far enough away, we'll still be able to do it."

"That's great," I said, lifting my glass in salute. "Have fun."

"You guys doing anything tonight?" my son asked.

"Nah," I answered, realizing my words were a bit more slurred than I cared for. "Just hangin' out, staying dry." I couldn't pull my head away from what it would be like to get home and have to keep things with Ben a secret.

I wasn't sure I could do it.

But if he couldn't even bring himself to let my son see us sitting close on the patio, what hope was there for a relationship at home?

To be fair, a conversation with the kids might be in order before they just see you together after Ben's given you the boning of a lifetime.

I snorted again, trying my best to cover it, but the looks on Ben's and Jason's faces said I'd done a poor job of it.

After a bit more small talk, Jason said goodbye, and I put down the drink.

"You okay?" Ben asked, a flash of guilt lighting up his face.

"Yeah, just don't need any more of that. I'm buzzed."

He was quiet for a while, but he eventually joined me on the couch. "Sorry about that, he took me by surprise."

I hummed, keeping my eyes closed against the spinning. "S'okay," I murmured. "Think I'm gonna go sleep. That last one hit me hard. Still wanna scuba dive tomorrow?"

"Yeah, sounds good," Ben answered, a world of regret and confusion in his words.

You and me both, I thought as I took my buzzed, sleepy self to the bathroom.

By the time I flopped into bed and curled protectively in on myself, my brain was at war.

Give him time. He's never been in a same-sex relationship. He might not adjust overnight.

No. If he can't acknowledge what we have now, you can't expect that will change once you're back home. You deserve better. You're forty-eight, you're not going back in the closet. No matter how gorgeous and perfect he seems.

That night was the first terrible sleep I got since stepping foot on the island.

Morning dawned warm and bright, the storm from the night before forgotten. Ben's arm was heavy draped across me and I smiled at the memories of our day spent stuck in the hut.

"Morning," he mumbled, rolling close for a kiss.

I pushed him away with a groan. "God, no. My mouth tastes like death. Let me brush my teeth first."

"What time is scuba diving?" Ben asked, his hand roaming up and down my back.

"Not 'til afternoon, why?"

"Just wondering if we had time for you to ride me before we headed out."

My cock immediately jumped on board and I chuckled. "Pretty sure that can be arranged." His behavior around Jason last night still stung, but we'd known what we were doing when we started a fling with only two weeks in paradise. I'd deal with the consequences of my actions once we were back home.

After a thorough shower and brushing my teeth, I joined Ben back in bed.

We definitely had time for a ride.

And my hips would probably protest all damn day.

But what a way to start the morning.

The rest of our two weeks in paradise was absolutely perfect. Even with shadowy doubts creeping up on me from time-to-time, I couldn't help the grin splitting my face from ear-to-ear with each passing day I got to spend with Ben.

Our days were filled with island adventures. We went scuba diving twice, rented scooters again, took a deep-sea fishing trip, helped judge a sandcastle contest, attempted to learn how to surf—failed miserably—and walked to the tide pools almost every day.

We also took a couple island-themed cooking classes, signed up for three sunrise yoga sessions, and basically ate and drank our way around the island.

Daytime in paradise was filled with easy laughter, lots of fun, and getting to know each other on a level I never would have guessed I'd even *want* to know Ben Stephens before we stepped foot on the island.

Nighttime?

Our nights were also for getting to know each other, but on a whole different scale. Nights were filled with sex and it ranged from the most gentle, soft, slow lovemaking that nearly brought me to tears every time to hard, fast, kinky fucking that absolutely blew my damn mind.

And through it all, I couldn't help but think about how quickly Ben had moved away from my side when Jason walked into our hut.

We were close to going home and I had absolutely no clue how transitioning from paradise to our regular, everyday lives was going to go.

At forty-eight, I knew I should just talk to Ben about my concerns. But my anxiety got in the way—I didn't want to lose out on the last bit of time we had together if he was going to tell me he couldn't do a real relationship once we got back home.

He said he wanted to see where things could go my brain was fond of reminding me. I couldn't help but think maybe he meant see where things could go *while keeping it all under wraps.*

I knew we'd *have* to talk. I couldn't face the flight home and slipping back into my day-to-day without *knowing* where Ben stood.

Where *we* stood.

But that didn't mean I couldn't wait until our very last night on the island to face the truth.

TWELVE

"THE KIDS SAID they'd meet us on the beach for dinner,"
Reggie said as he scrolled through his phone. He was
stretched out on our bed, naked and beautiful, his skin
still dewy from his post-sex shower.

We'd been making the most of our time in paradise.
Island adventures during the day and mind-blowing sex
at night, but I knew I'd screwed up when I pulled away
from Reggie the evening Jason came to the hut.

I would have given anything to have that moment
back so I could do it the way I really wanted to. But in
that moment, with nothing to prepare me for one of our
kids walking in on us, I'd let fear and uncertainty
overtake me.

I hated that I'd hurt Reggie or made him doubt what I
felt for him.

But a tiny part of me wondered if he really wanted to
deal with my issues once we got back home. Our time on
the island had been a great escape, but I still had a shit-
ton of baggage and a lifetime of bad experiences to work

through. Maybe that was more than Reggie had bargained for.

I needed to talk to him. *We* needed to talk. About the kids. What we imagined for *us* when we got back home. If there was even going to be an us. I thought I'd shown my hand clearly enough that Reggie would know I was interested in seeing where things went, but I also knew a person's anxiety could convince them of things that just weren't true. So, yeah, we needed to talk.

We carried all the makings for drinks to a little fire pit on the beach. It was our last night on the island and we were having an ocean-side dinner with Jason and Megan. Tara and Matt had flown out earlier in the day, and the four of us had a flight the next day. An easy, casual dinner, suggested by our kids, had sounded like the perfect way to end our two weeks in paradise.

Reggie set to work arranging the chairs and preparing drinks as I built the fire in the pit. "I think I'll miss the sound of the waves most of all," he said wistfully.

"Yeah, me too," I said. "We'll have the warmth all summer, I'll be bitching about the heat, but the constant comforting sound of the water will be missed."

My phone buzzed with a text.

Megan: Picking up the food. They're running late. Be there soon.

"Kids are getting the food, but place is running late." I filled Reggie in. "Might as well start with drinks."

"As long as we don't have hangovers to take home with us. I get anxious enough flying, I don't need to add a headache and nausea to it."

We settled in on the two chairs closest together, overlooking the fire, and watched as the sun inched closer and closer to the horizon.

Reaching over, I took Reggie's hand.

His eyes zeroed in on our joined fingers and then met mine. "The kids will be here soon," he whispered.

"That's okay," I answered.

"What are we doing?" he asked.

It was a simple question and I could have taken the easy way out with a flippant answer about enjoying our last night on the island with our children or something equally obtuse.

Instead, I smiled and caressed my thumb over his. "What do you think the kids will think when they find out?"

Reggie shook his head. "Truthfully? I have no idea. I'd like to think they'll be happy. Or at least indifferent. But part of me worries they'll be creeped out about it."

I nodded. "I've had a lot of the same thoughts."

We sipped our drinks and watched the waves.

After a moment, Reggie prompted, "And?"

"I've never really seen good examples of loving relationships. Once, a man came in the shop to commission a piece for his wife. It was a dining room table and chairs. He rambled on about how it was a beast of a project and a huge expense, but he gave me a wink and said, 'But when you find the other half of your heart, you end up doing stuff you never thought you'd do.' That stuck with me because it made no sense to me. My parents didn't have that. I never saw that with any couples in the church. Lariah and I definitely didn't have that." I paused and sipped my drink, taking in the gorgeous sunset. "When Megan fell for Jason, I got a hint of it, but it wasn't the same seeing my child experience it."

Reggie squeezed my hand. "They really do love each other," he mused.

"They do," I agreed. "Maybe this is too much," I started.

"I thought worrying and overthinking was my job," Reggie teased, breaking up some of the tension.

Chuckling, I went on, "These two weeks started out a bit bumpy, but being forced to get to know you was the best thing that ever happened to me. I don't know what's going to happen when we get back home—hell, maybe you don't want the same thing I do—but I know what that guy meant now. I always wondered what it would feel like when soulmates found their way to each other, when two halves met up and discovered they were one whole..." I took a breath. "And then I spent two weeks in paradise with you."

We were silent for several heartbeats.

When Reggie wiped a tear and leaned over to kiss me, I cupped his face, swiping away more tears and bringing our lips together. Tender heat bloomed as our mouths mated, expressing feelings our words just couldn't give justice to.

"I told you it would work," a very familiar voice crowed from behind us.

Reggie jerked away from me, wiping a hand over his mouth, eyes wide. "Oh, um..." He trailed off, a desperate look on his face.

Not that I could blame him for not knowing how to respond. I'd basically dumped him off my lap when Jason came in the other night. Now, both Megan and Jason had seen us kissing. He was probably wondering how I was going to play it off. And that was fair.

We hadn't really gotten to the point in our discussion over *how* we'd tell the kids, or even *if* we'd tell them.

Clinging to the deal Reggie and I had made early on, I dove head-first and took control. Reaching for Reggie's hand, I leaned in to kiss his cheek. "We've got this. Even if we have to make adjustments later, I'm not going to deny what we have."

His eyes shimmered in the warm glow of the sinking sun and flames from the fire pit, and he nodded.

"Well, we hadn't quite gotten to the planning phase of how to tell you," I started, my heart nearly thumping out of my chest as Jason and Megan moved to face us. "I guess we've got a lot to tell you." I glanced at my daughter. "I guess I have a lot to tell *you* about who I am." The tension eased slightly when the kids gave easy smiles and Reggie squeezed my hand. "But we're not hiding. I spent most of my life being scared to be myself, not allowed to make decisions or have opinions. Getting to know Reggie opened up a world I'd never even let myself dream of. We want to be respectful of your feelings on this, but we're together. Yeah, we maybe can't promise forever, but we'd like to have you on our side as we figure things out." The words escaped me in a whoosh, leaving me deflated and wary as I watched Jason and Megan take in what I'd said.

After a few moments, Reggie grunted. "Wait, what did you mean *I told you it would work*? What would work?"

Megan grinned her megawatt sunshine smile. Jason just smirked and rolled his eyes.

"She means I owe her fifty bucks and I'm doing dishes for a month because *I* thought it would take more than just two weeks in paradise to get you two together. But," he paused and put his arm around my daughter, kissing her cheek, "my dear wife is smarter than me in every single way, and *she* said we only had to make sure you two were stuck together enough times. She bet me fifty dollars and a month of dishes that you'd be together before we left the island." Jason chucked. "And damn if she wasn't right."

"Whhaatt?" Reggie drawled. "You two little shits planned this whole thing?"

"The seats on the plane? The whole *there's only one hut*? The two-seater scooter? All of it?" I asked, struggling to conceal my shock, but loving the grin of extreme joy on my daughter's face.

Megan gave a little shrug before dipping into a sweeping bow. "I believe the words you're both looking for are *thank you*," she said with a giggle. "My work here is done and I will greatly enjoy a month of no dishes." She tapped her chin. "Hmmmm, where will I spend my fifty dollars?"

"How did you know?" I asked.

"How did I know that my dad, the man who loved and protected me my entire life, was broken and lonely because of a shitty past, thought he'd probably never find the right person to love, but just needed a push in the right direction toward someone who needed him just as much?" Megan asked.

Reggie's eyes met mine and we smiled.

"Yeah, how did you know all of that?" I asked.

She shrugged again. "I'm good and I took a leap of faith the tension and sidelong glances between the two of you would spark into something more if just given the chance. Plus, you're both good-looking guys for your age, *and* you're just *good* people. It was kinda a no-brainer."

Reggie squeezed my hand and I wondered if he was thinking the same thing I was. *Not to mention you both had some kinks that lined up perfectly.* I bit my lip, positive the kids wouldn't want to hear about *that*, no matter how happy they were for us.

The four of us settled in for dinner and drinks as the sun sank below the horizon and the waves lapped at the shore. Two weeks in paradise had started with me tense and fearful of losing my little girl. Our last night in paradise ended with my heart full because I'd gained so much more.

THIRTEEN

Reggie

"Look at me," Ben demanded, his hand cupping my chin and forcing my eyes up to meet his in the mirror as his cock slammed into me over and over. "That's it, watch me fuck my little cum slut."

My body shuddered, bent over the low dresser, my legs spread, one propped on the flat surface. The position opened me up for Ben's cock and he took full advantage of it. Grateful the hut was free-standing with no neighbors to hear us through the walls, I cried out as Ben's balls slapped against me, his thick cock sliding in and out of my hole. "Oh god, Ben," I whimpered. "Give it to me, please."

I clenched my ass around his shaft as I begged for his load, loving the way Ben grunted and fucked me harder. He bent at the waist, his chest pressing to my back, and gripped my chin again. "Tell me what you want, you dirty little cock whore. Beg for it."

With our eyes locked, I licked my lips, focusing on the slick, hot flesh impaling my tight channel. "Please,

Ben. Fill me up, give me your load. Come in me. Breed me," I chanted, the words spilling from my lips in rhythm to his thrusting cock.

As the edge of the dresser bit into my hips, Ben's broad chest plastered to my sweaty back, and my balls drew up tight, I never once took my eyes from his. The air, fragrant with tropical flowers, sea salt, and sunshine, filled with the sounds of our coupling. I took it all in—the full, slick sensation of Ben spreading me open; the scent of our sex and sweat; the smack of flesh against flesh.

We'd awakened earlier than necessary the morning of our flight home, both of us seeming determined to spend our last moments in paradise enjoying each other's body. Sure, we had all the time in the world once we got back home, but we could sleep on the plane, one last chance to be bred in paradise wasn't something I could pass up.

When my balls emptied themselves, my orgasm spilling over my fist, Ben grunted and slammed his hips into me, unloading his cum deep in my hole. When his cock eventually stopped pulsing, he slipped from my body and stepped slightly to the side. Wrapping an arm around my chest, Ben hefted me slightly upright and devoured my mouth as he pressed his thumb against my destroyed hole.

"Mmmm," he murmured against my lips. "Sweet little hole is dripping my cum like the good little cum slut you are." He chuckled evilly when my greedy hole clenched around his thumb. "That's right, you dirty cum hole, show me how much you like Daddy's load filling you up." With the pad of his thumb, Ben pushed the slick wetness back into my ass.

I whimpered, my body shaking.

"Who owns this ass? Who gets to breed this pretty little hole?"

"You," I sobbed, my knees giving out, only Ben's strong arm holding me up as he pushed his cum back into my leaking hole over and over. "God, Ben, only you."

"That's right, no one else gets to fill this tight little pucker with his load. This cum slut belongs to me."

My cock gave a final twitch and I opened my mouth for Ben's seeking tongue.

By the time we broke for air, took showers, and carried our bags to the boat, I was exhausted, exhilarated, and excited to get home.

There were no guarantees, but I was looking forward to what Ben and I might build together from the seeds we planted in paradise.

"I'm sorry, sirs," the airline employee said from behind her counter. "Due to the mechanical issue on *your* flight, we've moved as many people as possible to another flight. We've reached the limit of passengers on this flight."

Jason and Megan threw us a worried look as they glanced toward the gate where the cheerful attendant was hurrying the last few passengers through the door.

"Go," Ben said to our kids. "We'll get home. You both have plans tomorrow so you need to get on that plane." We'd taken two flights to get to the boat on the way down, but thought we'd lucked out with a non-stop flight on the way home.

No such luck.

Megan and Jason had been the last passengers from our canceled flight offered seats on the other plane heading home.

The kids looked torn, but they gave us quick hugs and rushed toward the gate.

"What are our other options?" Ben asked the employee behind the counter.

"Well," the person grimaced as they clicked the keys. "I hate to say it, but I don't know that there's a flight going anywhere near your home airport until tomorrow night. Now, there *is* a flight leaving in the morning that would take you a couple states over and you could possibly catch a flight home from there."

I took a deep breath, my anxiety skyrocketing, a meltdown threatening. Just as I was about to either let loose a string of anxiety-induced complaints or curl myself into a corner and cry, Ben put his arm around my shoulders and pulled me close. With a tight squeeze to ground me, he continued speaking to the employee while I did my best to focus more on the options and less on the fact we were holding up the line and getting nasty comments from other angry passengers behind us.

"Maybe we think outside of the box for a minute," Ben said. "What are our other options?"

"I'm sorry, sir, the flights available—"

"No, outside of the box. Your plane had a mechanical issue. The non-stop flight we paid for to get us home is no longer an option and you've run out of other solutions regarding flying us home. So, what can you do for us to ensure we get home?" Ben asked, his voice calm and firm.

"Well, sir, depending on how quickly you need to get home—" the employee started.

"We need to get home when we get home—as quickly as possible, but we'd rather not be stuck in this airport or another while *hoping* there's a flight that would lead to another terrible layover. You tell us what you can do, we'll decide which is the better plan for our needs."

"Taxi vouchers? We could probably get you into a taxi that would drive you home," the airline employee, Raye, said hesitantly.

"Okay, now we're talking. That's a start. What else?"

Raye wrinkled their nose. "Rental car and a hotel?"

Ben bumped a fist on the counter. "That sounds promising. Tell me more."

"We can provide a rental that you can drop off at home, a hotel for a night, and gift cards to a couple restaurants."

"That works," Ben said, sounding triumphant. "Let's do it."

An hour later, we had our rental loaded up, a reservation at a hotel seven hours away, and two gift cards for decent restaurants. If we pushed it, we'd only need one night in a hotel, but Ben had already mentioned maybe we'd just make a road trip of it. The thought of a couple nights on the road with Ben, stopping at little out-of-the-way diners and antique stores wasn't terrible.

Even though we both *did* have jobs to get back to.

"Whatdya think?" Ben asked as he pulled the rental onto the road. "Stop tonight and push it tomorrow to get back home around midnight? Or stop tonight since we've got a free room. Drive until we want to stop tomorrow, stay somewhere, drive the rest of the way the day after?"

"Both sound like decent options," I said. "Maybe we see what we feel like tomorrow?" Even if we'd been able to keep our non-stop flight, our home was two hours away from the closest airport. Either trip would have been exhausting, but I figured the tiny road trip with Ben was better than being stuck on a plane or sleeping in an airport.

That night, despite a seven-hour drive, we ordered Chinese, showered, and spent the night exploring each other's bodies in the king-sized bed.

"Oh fuck, Reggie," Ben growled, his hand fisted in my hair, guiding my mouth up and down on his cock while I worked a dildo in and out of his ass and teased his tightly pebbled nipples with my fingers.

I loved spreading him open, playing with his nipples, and swallowing his cock. He'd already fucked me into the mattress earlier, so I'd made it a goal to make him come with my mouth, fingers, and the toy.

"Fuck, fuck, fuck," he chanted, thrusting hard and fast into my mouth, knowing how much I loved choking on his cock. "Such a hungry little cum slut. You gonna swallow Daddy's load?"

Moaning around his shaft, I took him deep, thrusting the silicone against his prostate, and pinching a nipple hard.

Ben tensed and grunted, his hot, thick release pulsing onto my tongue. Letting his throbbing cock slip from my mouth, I moved to dribble his cum onto his nipples before sucking it off, swirling my tongue around the tight flesh as Ben rocked himself on the dildo.

Later, after showers, we slept curled together.

When we woke, the morning was already late and the thought of driving straight through was less than desirable.

"We have an hour before we have to check out," Ben murmured against my cheek, his hand trailing down my chest to cup my morning wood.

"I think I've created a monster," I teased, thrusting against the palm of his hand. "What did you have in mind?"

"Well," Ben nibbled my ear. "This hotel is *nice*. The one we stay at tonight will be on the cheaper end..."

"We're staying over tonight? Not that I mind..."

"Not ready to give up sleeping with you in my arms," Ben mumbled.

"First, I'm all for sleepovers," I said, trying to keep things light, but thinking I could *easily* move out of my apartment.

Whoa, down boy. No one said anything about moving in together.

Yeah, but it would be very easy.

Just sayin'.

"Second, what does this place being *nice* have to do with anything?"

"We have a balcony," Ben said, his words husky.

"A balcony with neighbors that looks out over a parking lot, a road, and faces another building," I said, just the thought of possibly being watched thickening my cock as I spoke.

"Wanna fuck my little cum slut out there," Ben said. "The neighbors might hear, but the walls between our balconies will hide us. Anyone who sees us or hears us will know I own this ass."

"Fuck, Ben," I groaned.

"You in?"

"Yessss," I hissed. "Fuck, yes."

The morning wasn't as warm as paradise, but the soft breeze was nice and the sun burned down on our balcony.

"Bend over the railing, show Daddy that pretty little hole," Ben demanded.

Spreading my legs, I bent at the waist. Gasping at the slick finger coating my hole with lube, I gripped the railing. "Fuck, Ben, give it to me."

He pushed into me in one long thrust, making me cry out. Ben took hold of my hips and railed me, hard and fast. The people and cars below were small, but I could see them well enough—which meant they could see me if they just looked up. My dick pulsed at the thought of someone watching Ben own my ass.

"Ride me," Ben demanded. "Sit on my cock and take my cum." He pulled out and moved to the lounge chair. Spread out before me like a damn buffet, Ben stroked his dick and beckoned for me to straddle him.

Doing as I was told, loving every second of Ben's command, I straddled him and lowered myself onto his cock. When I bottomed out, I pulled Ben into a sitting position. Playing with his nipples as I thrust my tongue between his lips, I rocked my hips and took his cock deep. Breaking the kiss only because we both needed to breathe, I whispered against his mouth, "Anyone can see us. Show them how you breed me. Fill me with your babies."

My words spurred Ben on and he rocked up into me, pegging my prostate with each deep thrust. "Jack yourself, come on me," Ben demanded.

The door next door opened and a man's voice, seemingly talking on the phone, sounded. He continued his conversation for a moment, but then Ben thrust deep and I cried out.

"Good God," the man said. "I think the people next door are fucking on the balcony." He chuckled at whatever the person on the phone said. Then we heard the click of a lighter and cigarette smoke wafted over the wall. "Nah, sounds like they're having a good ol' time. More fun than me."

Turning my focus back to Ben, I took hold of my cock and stroked.

"That's a good boy," Ben said, gripping my hips so hard I knew I'd have bruises. "Ride Daddy's cock."

I whimpered, jacking myself hard and fast, my balls drawing up tight as an orgasm built.

"Tell me, Reg, tell me what you want," Ben demanded.

"Give me your cum," I gasped. "Breed me."

The late morning sun warmed our bodies as the air echoed with the sounds of our sex. When I painted stripes of cum across Ben's chest, he slammed up into me, his cock pulsing as he shot his load deep in my ass.

As we came down from our high, a familiar sound floated across the balcony wall. The neighbor hissed and grunted and I had no doubt he'd just jacked off after hearing Ben and me fucking.

"That was fuckin' hot," the neighbor said before he moaned and fell silent. His phone rang and he answered. "What? Oh, yeah, lost connection there for a second. Huh? Yeah, I guess they finished. Mmhm, I've got the notes for the meeting, not a problem." The sliding door opened and our neighbor's voice faded away.

"That was hot as hell," Ben said, pressing kisses against my chest.

"Guess we can firmly add exhibitionism to our kinks," I said with a chuckle as I lifted myself off Ben's cock.

Six hours later, I groaned as Ben pulled into a chain hotel.

"Let's order food the second we know our room number," he said. "I'm fuckin' starving."

We threw our bags on one bed, flopped onto the second bed, ordered our food, and then spent twenty of the thirty minutes for delivery making out in the shower.

After finishing our dinner, Ben looked out the window. "Want to go for a walk?"

"To where?"

"There's a little pond back there," he said, taking my hand and leading me toward the door. "Let's go, I need to walk off my food."

I laughed. "It's like fifty feet from the parking lot."

"We'll walk it three times," Ben said, throwing his arm around my shoulders.

When we reached the little pond, moonlight reflecting from the calm surface and frogs croaking a nighttime lullaby, Ben pulled me down to sit with him on a bench. He turned to face me, took my hands in his, and blew out a nervous breath.

"What's going on?" I asked.

"I know it's too fast, but I also know it's the most real feeling I've ever had," Ben started. "I've never known love. Never been in love. And I don't want to ignore this." He caressed my knuckles and blew out another breath. "I love you." He huffed. "I'm in love with you."

My heart caught in my chest, my breath hitching as I allowed his words to wash over me. "I'm not too much? Over-the-top? Drama you don't want to deal with?"

Ben shook his head and pressed his lips to my knuckles. "No. You woke me up, helped me find the real Ben. He was buried so deep, I thought he was dead, but you uncovered him." He leaned in to kiss me. "Just wish it hadn't taken us so long to find each other."

"No, I think this is the way it needed to be. We had a lot of living and learning to do. Not that I would have wanted you to go through what you did, but our pasts made us who we are today. Gave us Megan and Jason. We needed to live through all of that to become the Ben and Reggie we are today. Twenty or thirty years ago wasn't our time. Those guys back then weren't ready for what we've found. We can't regret the past, just look forward to the future."

"God, I love you," Ben whispered fiercely.

Brushing my lips over his, I grinned. "I love you, too."

"Now, you wanna risk arrest for public indecency in a city park? Or you wanna spread your sexy little hole open for me in our bed?" Ben asked, already pulling me to stand.

I knew we'd eventually get home from our two weeks in paradise, but I wasn't going to complain about hot, kinky sex with the man I loved as we made our way there.

Epilogue

BEN

One Year Later

"You sure you want to do this?" Reggie asked as we approached the cemetery.

"Yeah. It's time. Beyond time. I want it done before we leave," I said. Our suitcases sat packed and ready at the house we now shared—Reggie had moved in about six months after we returned from paradise.

We were leaving later that afternoon for a week in New York. Three Broadway shows were on the itinerary and Reggie was beside himself with excitement to show me some of his favorites.

I'd been attending every show Reggie performed in or had any part in the production of, but knowing we were going to see his favorites *on* Broadway was something special.

"Okay, I just don't want it to upset you," Reggie said, taking my hand as we drew closer to the headstone marked *Lariah Stephens*.

"It won't." I cleared my throat. "Bruce agrees I'm ready to do this. I've felt ready for quite a while. Megan already came out here to unload."

I chuckled at the thought of my daughter telling her mother's grave that she was going to spend the money Lariah left her on secular charities, especially focusing on abortion rights, gender-affirming care, and supporting LGBTQ+ teens.

"Megan said she could almost *hear* Lariah rolling over in her grave." Clearing my throat again, I looked down at the ornate headstone. I didn't feel a single ounce of sadness that my wife had died. I was quiet for a long time. "You nearly destroyed me," I whispered, the words rough. "Between you, the church, and our parents, I wasn't sure I was going to make it. I wouldn't have if I hadn't gotten out when I did. Not gonna let my Lariah show," I said with a chuckle, "so I'm not glad you suffered as badly as you did there at the end. I wouldn't want that for anyone." I squeezed Reggie's hand. "Everything in my past made me who I am today—made me stronger. You all tried to keep me down, tried to use me, but there were better things waiting for me. I want you to meet Reggie, the man I love. He's the most amazing person I've ever met and I'm so fucking head-over-heels in love with him it's not even funny. I'm sorry if someone hurt you in your past. I'd never wish that on anyone. You tried to bury me with your hatred, but I had something to live for—even if I didn't know it back then. The hate you showed me helped me recognize true love when it came knocking. So, I guess I can say thank you for that." I tucked Reggie under my arm and held him close. "Megan is happy and healthy, despite you. *I'm* happy and healthy, despite you, the church, and my parents. It may have taken forty-nine years, but I'm embracing all of the good because I deserve it. I hope you can rest in peace. Or not," I said with a shrug. "I really don't give a fuck."

With a relieved laugh, I blew out a long breath.

"You good?" Reggie asked.

I nodded. "Yeah. I'm better than good."

We walked toward the car, but I took a detour to a little bridge across a creek.

"Babe, we're kinda on a schedule," Reggie warned, a touch of anxiety creeping into his voice.

"Shhh, this won't take long." I walked him to the middle of the bridge. "I was going to do this in New York. Or maybe take you back to the island, but I can't wait."

His eyes sparkled with curiosity and I was reminded again why I loved this man so very much.

"Do you remember that night in paradise when we talked about whether either of us would ever want to get married again?"

Reggie nodded.

"I still don't know if I could ever get married again," I said.

His expression remained soft and focused on my words, but I thought I saw a flash of sadness in his eyes.

"But that doesn't mean I don't want to spend the rest of my life loving someone, sharing my life with him, and building new memories to replace the old," I added quickly, the words catching in my throat. "We both know we're not promised tomorrow." I took a deep breath. "If you'll have me, and you're okay with exchanging vows without the piece of paper," I dug into my pocket and pulled out a ring, "I'd like to ask you to spend the rest of our lives together."

Reggie hiccupped a sob and nodded.

Taking his hand and slipping the ring onto his finger, I said, "Reggie Ward, I promise to love you, keep you grounded when you need it, soothe your anxiety, and support you in your journey of just being *you*." I kissed him. "Guess what I'm saying is *I love you, let's live our forevers together until we no longer can*."

"Our very own happy for now," Reggie said with a smile. He took a deep breath. "I don't have a ring for you."

Chuckling, I took a second ring out of my pocket and handed it to him. He smiled broadly and slipped it on my finger.

"Had I known we were exchanging vows, I would have—"

I cut him off with a kiss. "Had you known we were exchanging vows, you would have been a blob of worry. I took that part out of the equation."

He laughed through tears. "And I love you for that." Clearing his throat, he said, "For the record, I don't need a piece of paper to prove my commitment to you." He took both of my hands in his. "Ben Stephens, I love you and I will spend the rest of our lives proving to you just how much. I will support you through the good times and the bad. I will gladly let you ground me and take control. I will spend vacations with you on Broadway, in paradise, and anywhere else our hearts take us. I'll explore kinks with you, but I'll forever be more than happy with good ol' sweet and steamy," he said with a smirk.

Pulling him into my arms, I tipped Reggie's chin and kissed him to seal our vows.

What started as two weeks in paradise sure did look like forever.

~The End~

Want more addictive, sexy, emotional M/M romance?
Find **On Cravenwood Block** HERE
or all other A.D. Ellis books at Amazon.
Want to stay up-to-date?
Subscribe to A.D.'s newsletter.
Want to say thanks and support my writing, plus get some special extras for being a subscriber?
Check out my Ream page HERE.

Also by A. D. Ellis

Jett & Leighton: On Cravenwood Block- a steamy, opposites-attract, bisexual-awakening, roommates-to-lovers M/M romance featuring a sexy-as-sin tattoo artist and a fresh, flashy barista with a smile that lights up the room.

Ollie & Bash: On Cravenwood Block- a steamy, opposites-attract, roommates-to-lovers, boss/employee, age-gap M/M romance featuring a man not looking for love and a younger music director with no filter.

Julian & Shaw: On Cravenwood Block- a steamy, hurt/comfort, roommates-to-lovers, age-gap M/M romance featuring an apartment manager with a heart of gold and a younger man doing his best to heal from a traumatic past.

Holly Hills Christmas- Holly Hills Christmas is a steamy, feel-good, M/M age-gap holiday romance.

The Perfect Blend- A steamy, M/M age-gap, marriage of convenience, coffee shop romance

Perfect Timing is a steamy, M/M romance with an introverted, demisexual writer and a big, soft teddy bear of a nurse trying to navigate a love they've always dreamed of but most definitely weren't expecting.

Adore (Remington Place 1) is a steamy, age-gap, bi-awakening, dad's best friend M/M romance with a sassy smartass and a sexy silver fox. It's the first book in the Remington Place series and can be read as a stand-alone.

Crave (Remington Place 2) is a steamy, friends-to-lovers, fake relationship M/M romance with a virgin nursing student and a gruff, grumbly construction worker.

Desire (Remington Place 3) is a steamy, age-gap, hurt/comfort M/M romance featuring a heart-of-gold mechanic and a twink who's a lot stronger than he realizes. *Please note: This story has mention of sex trafficking and sexual abuse.*

Yearn (Remington Place 4)- a steamy, enemies-to-lovers, forced proximity M/M romance between two EMS workers who have hated each other for a decade.

Power Struggle is a steamy M/M, age-gap, forced proximity romance set in a small town. A twenty-year history, rival schools and jobs, and a hotel with only one bed make for a hot and heavy, sweet and sexy, HEA-guaranteed love story.

Take Me Home M/M age-gap, opposites-attract romance with plenty of steam and a scene that will make you appreciate camouflage and work boots

Let Love In M/M age-gap, forced proximity, dad's best friend, bisexual-awakening romance. Available on AUDIO!

Let Love Win M/M brother's best friend romance. Available on AUDIO!

Buried Secrets Romantic suspense stand-alone title. Available on AUDIO!

Silver in the City (3 books- meet the Silver crew you read about in Forged in the City) Available on AUDIO!

Forged in the City (3 books- a spin-off series from Silver in the City) Available on AUDIO

The BJ Boys Series (3 books, small town, big love) Available on AUDIO

Forever Better Together (friends to lovers) Available on AUDIO!

His Reluctant Cowboy (age gap, opposites attract, cowboy romance) Available on AUDIO!

What Blooms Beneath (LGBT Fantasy romance) Available on AUDIO!

Sawyer

(this was the first M/M I wrote and you may remember Sawyer and Luke being mentioned in <u>Barrett & Ivan</u> as well as in <u>Ryker & Gavin</u>)

The <u>Something About Him</u> series has been revamped with revised stories, updated blurbs, and spiffy new covers.

The series is available on ALL of your favorite book platforms!

Bryan & Jase

Brody & Nick

Barrett & Ivan

Braeton & Drew

Ryker & Gavin

Kade & Cameron

A.D.'s first stories (all male/female except Sawyer which is male/male) are in the Torey Hope and Torey Hope: The Later Years series. Find the 8 book box set HERE or you can find each individual title on Amazon.

For Nicky

Because of Beckett

Christmas in Torey Hope

Loving Josie

Decker

Sawyer

Zach

Kendrick

About the Author

A.D. Ellis is an Indiana girl, born and raised. She spends much of her time in central Indiana as an instructional coach/teacher in the inner city of Indianapolis, being a mom to two amazing teenagers, and wondering how she and her husband of over two decades haven't driven each other insane yet. A lot of her time is also devoted to phone call avoidance and her hatred of cooking.

She loves chocolate, wine, pizza, and naps along with reading and writing romance. These loves don't leave much time for housework, much to the chagrin of her husband. Who would pick cleaning the house over a nap or a good book? She uses any extra time to increase her fluency in sarcasm.

A.D. uses she/they pronouns.

Want to say thanks, support my writing, or get special extras for subscribers? Check out my Ream page HERE.

Sign up at http://www.subscribepage.com/ADEllisNewsMMRomance for a FREE books!

Website http://adellisauthor.com/

Find me EVERYWHERE at https://www.adellisauthor.com/mylinks/

Connect with A.D. Ellis

Follow my website http://www.adellisauthor.com or find me on Facebook

http://www.facebook.com/adellisauthor

If you want to get updates about releases, interviews, sales, giveaways, and more please sign up for my newsletter http://www.subscribepage.com/ADEllisNewsMMRomance

Check out my TikTok- https://www.tiktok.com/@adellisauthor

You can also find me on Twitter http://www.twitter.com/ADEllisAuthor

Find me on Spotify if you'd like to listen to the playlist for this book (mainly just the songs I listened to while writing). Just search for A.D. Ellis.

To make it easy, find me EVERYWHERE here-https://www.adellisauthor.com/mylinks/

Acknowledgments

It's always so hard to write this part because I'm worried I'll forget someone without meaning to.

Readers- you are the reason I write. As long as you continue reading my stories, I'll continue writing them. Thank you for your support.

Bloggers- your support, reviews, and promotion are very much appreciated. Thank you!

My author buddies- I don't know that I could keep doing this without our brainstorm sessions, laughter, road trips, meals, wine, and friendship as my support.

Thank you to my alpha readers, betas, editors, proofreaders, and ARC readers! Your eyes and input are beyond important to me.

Brett and Gage- as usual, I doubt you even grasp how much your support, input, and friendship mean to me. This author journey has brought many wonderful things into my life, and you both are two of the BEST! I'm blessed to call you friends.

My family and friends- thank you for your love and support, always.